The Shrine

AND OTHER STORIES

Also by Mary Lavin

Novels
THE HOUSE IN CLEWE STREET
MARY O'GRADY

Short Stories
TALES FROM BECTIVE BRIDGE
THE LONG AGO
THE BECKER WIVES
AT SALLYGAP
THE LIKELY STORY
A SINGLE LADY
THE PATRIOT SON
THE GREAT WAVE
SELECTED STORIES
IN THE MIDDLE OF THE FIELDS
HAPPINESS
COLLECTED STORIES
A MEMORY

The Shrine

AND OTHER STORIES
BY
MARY LAVIN

Houghton Mifflin Company Boston

1977

First American Edition

Copyright © 1977 by Mary Lavin

Library of Congress Cataloging in Publication Data

Lavin, Mary, date
    The shrine, and other stories.
    CONTENTS: The shrine.—Tom.—The mug of water.—
Senility.—Eterna.
    I. Title.
PZ3.L393Sh 1977 [PR6023.A914]   823'.9'12
77-24044
ISBN 0-395-25773-5

Printed in the United States of America

S 10 9 8 7 6 5 4 3 2 1

The story "Tom" originally appeared in *The New Yorker*,
January 1973; "Eterna" appeared in *The New Yorker* in
March 1976. "A Mug of Water" was first published in
Southern Review, April 1974. "The Shrine" originally ap-
peared in *Sewanee Review*, Spring 1974.

For Mick and Caroline

Contents

The Shrine

AND OTHER STORIES

The Shrine

Next morning the Canon's housekeeper brought Mary her breakfast in bed and, much as she hated to think of the old woman lumbering up the stairs with the heavy tray, Mary was glad not to have to face her uncle until later in the morning. By then, if her fiancé did as he intended, he would have gone traipsing off over the countryside. And, left alone with the Canon, she could try to patch up last night's unfortunate quarrel. She had heard the Canon going out to say early Mass and she'd heard his car crunching the gravel under her window on his return. But she had not heard Don go down. Had he given up his plan? She half hoped he had. She was afraid to think what her uncle would say if he found out what was in Don's mind.

Then, as she was pouring a second cup of tea, Mary heard voices below raised in a brief but sharp exchange. Next minute the front door closed. Springing out of bed and going to the window, she was in time to see Don hitting out across the fields in the direction of the Shrine. She sighed. If the two men had continued their argument this morning nothing would save the weekend. Damn the Shrine anyway, she thought. If only she hadn't let her uncle inveigle them into going there last night when Don and she were both tired after the long drive from Dublin.

The meal old Ellen had prepared for them was very good, and while they were eating it the two men seemed to be getting on famously. If they'd sat on at the table a little longer, even the Canon himself might have been unwilling to stir out. But she herself had been anxious to get the visit to the Shrine over and done with, and it seemed a good idea to go down at that hour when the booths and stalls would, she thought, be closed up and shuttered for the night. She hadn't realized that it was Lady Day, and that business would be going full blast until the final busload of pilgrims left with the traders' touts running alongside the departing coaches in a frantic effort to sell one more statue, one more holy-water font, one more medal.

When they arrived at the Shrine it was blazing with candles, and the yard around the relatively inoffensive church had the festive air of a bazaar. She'd seen Don staring with disgust at one booth where gigantic bunches of rosary beads hung down between brown scapulars. 'Like overripe berries,' she whispered, hoping to make light of the vulgarity. But Don didn't laugh. 'Poisonous berries', he retorted. And Mary glanced nervously at her uncle in case the old man might have overheard. At the time she couldn't have said whether it was fortunate or unfortunate when Mullins came running across from his new shop and started slobbering all over them. To her surprise the Canon, usually unsociable, accepted the fellow's invitation to go inside and have a glass of sherry – which was of course undrinkable – and she saw Don look at his glass as if he expected to see an engraving of the Virgin on it.

All the same, things might not have been too bad if Don had not already known about Mullins. To while away the time on the drive down from Dublin, she had told him how Mullins had been the first to set up a stall at the church gate after the Apparition, and how he had made so much money that he'd built his present premises opposite the grotto. Unfortunately she had also told Don about the other woman – the woman who had ousted his wife, who was now in a mental home.

'Is that the slut?' Don asked, quite audibly, as they passed through the shop on their way upstairs and saw the creature queening it behind the counter.

They only stayed a short while in Mullins's. Even the Canon couldn't stomach Mullins's sycophancy. Indeed the shopkeeper's eulogies of the proposed new basilica may well have been what triggered off their row later that evening. Mullins had a plaster-of-paris model of the proposed, and monstrously ugly, basilica on the counter of his shop with a money box in front of it. Needless to say he was chairman of the fund-raising committee.

And, when they were back in the parlour of the parochial house and Don asked the Canon innocently enough what he estimated the cost would be, Mary herself was staggered by the figure her uncle mentioned, but Don was fit to be tied.

'And where are you going to raise a sum like that?' Don cried. 'You're surely not going to dun it out of your poverty-stricken parishioners?'

'Not at all,' said the Canon airily. 'We're raising money all over Ireland, all over the world in fact. You'd be surprised how much is pouring in from England

and America – even Australia.' He looked quite pleased with himself until he remembered the word Don had used and his face went purple. 'Did you say "dun it out of people"?' After that the full fury of the row broke over her.

Oh, why did she bring Don down here in the first place? Why didn't she wait and let her uncle meet him on the day of the wedding? The old man was probably lonely enough at the thought of her marriage without being led to think, as he probably did now, that she was marrying an atheist. But her uncle's wedding present had been so generous she'd felt that the least she could do was to bring Don down and introduce him in advance. Not that she should have been surprised by his present, considering the long unbroken history of his generosity towards her ever since she was a child. Her mother was the Canon's only sister whom he had almost idolized, and, since her mother was a widow, he'd insisted on paying Mary's school fees and buying her books and her clothes. Indeed he used to buy her lots of little odds and ends that her mother could never have afforded. And when her mother died he virtually became her guardian. She had to be sent away to boarding school, of course, but she came to stay in the parochial house for all her school holidays. How he used to fuss about her! He was like a hen with one chick, making her change her clothes if she was out in the rain for a minute, and often insisting on drying her hair himself with a huge, and not always clean, towel of his own. As for the meals he provided! The fact that he was an ascetic himself did not prevent him from feeding her like a prize bantam. It was not only her physical welfare that concerned him, of course. He used to talk continually about modesty and purity, thinking that at her age she was too young to be embarrassed or to embarrass him. He probably thought that although she would not fully comprehend his veiled remarks, all the same something of his meaning would seep into her subconscious and when she was older his words might come back to her and be an armour against temptation – a breastplate to protect her from sin.

Poor Uncle! He must have been scared stiff when she'd first gone up to Dublin to the university, thinking she'd surely lose her virginity there. On the occasional week-end when she'd come down to visit him he always managed to drag a reference to the flesh into his sermon, making it clear that the Faith was the only prop that could be relied upon to keep the moral structure from collapse. And, as time went on, whenever she was in the congregation his sermon would be directed at her, as she sat where she'd always done, in the front pew, right under the pulpit.

'Innocence is like the bloom on a peach,' he'd intone, looking impersonally up at the organ loft. 'And when a rot sets in, it sets in at the core and works outward, slowly, so it is often a long time before the damage shows. This of course is part of the devil's clever plan. That gentleman always takes a private and personal delight in making his latest victim do his evil work for him. It is a common practice with him to see to it that the seduced becomes in turn the seducer.'

His sermons were mainly meant to be preventative, however, and if he found that one of his female parishioners had succumbed to a sin of the flesh he dropped his flowery talk pretty quickly and moved in decisively with great common sense to take action to prevent the girl from being what he referred to as 'pulped'. That crude word had always made Mary shudder. And what a sharp ear the old man had for discovering illicit pregnancies. In a matter of hours he'd have nipped the scandal in the bud and, with alarming dispatch, married off the offending girl. Whenever possible he married her to the father of the child, but if for any reason that was not possible, he'd unload her on to some ageing but compliant bachelor. At first Mary used to be shocked at the latter stratagem, but she was forced to admit the victims themselves usually thrived on his treatment. As well as providing a solution for the girls' problems, the marriages generally acted like a tonic on the old fellows and gave them a new lease of life. Frequently, girls thus hastened into wedlock ripened into pious matrons upon whom the Canon could later count for help in handling similar cases as they cropped up.

Mary had to smile as she reflected that there would have been no fear of her uncle's quarrelling with her fiancé if for one moment he'd thought there had been any hanky-panky, as he'd put it, between them. If he'd thought that was the case, he wouldn't have let any obstacle – not even Don's criticism of the Shrine – come between him and the speedy celebration of their nuptials. He would have seen to it that their plans were put forward and that they were married post-haste. Well, she had never given him grounds to worry about her on that score. She had never betrayed his trust in her. And, to give him his due, of late years he had never, or at least never before last night, shown the slightest anxiety about her in that respect. In her last year at college he had not only allowed her to go hitch-hiking on the Continent, knowing she'd be staying in youth hostels or cheap hotels, but had financed her trips, seeming as it were to participate in them vicariously by making out itineraries and route maps. His display of distrust last night was just an attempt to insult Don, albeit a well-calculated insult. When he and Don finally stopped arguing, long past midnight, and then only because they were all three exhausted as well as miserably unhappy, the old man stumped up the stairs in front of them and, after showing Don to his room, waited ostentatiously until the door closed on him before escorting her to her room. Outside her room, too, he stood waiting for her to close her door before trundling off to his own bed. As if she needed to be shown the way to the little room where she'd spent so many nights of her life. So many happy nights at that. But she forgave him. And, indeed, feeling certain Don would sneak down the corridor to say a private good-night to her, she stealthily opened her door again, just a crack, so there would be no need for him to knock. When she did hear him creeping along the landing she jumped out of bed and went to the door with her finger to her lips.

'Don't come in Don, please,' she begged.

'Why not?' Don asked roughly, but he glanced nervously at the Canon's door. 'He wouldn't come out, would he?' He seemed shaken at the thought.

'No, of course not. He wouldn't stoop to tactics like that, but we've upset him enough for one night,' she said. She was already afraid she would not sleep a wink for wondering whether the old man was lying awake in his uncomfortable bed, on the other side of the wall, castigating himself for imaginary failures on his part. 'Go back to your own room, Don, please,' she begged. All the same, catching him by the sleeve, she held him back for a second to ask if he still intended to go poking around the countryside. For he had managed as they came up the stairs to convey that he was going to do this; he had a hunch there could be mineral deposits in the area. Even though he was no expert, he wanted to poke around to see if there would be any justification for setting up further tests later. 'I hope my uncle doesn't know what you have in mind?' she asked anxiously.

'I don't care whether he knows or not,' Don said. 'Anyway, it's only a hunch. And if there should turn out to be minerals here, the old man couldn't but be pleased at the possibilities of prosperity there would be for his people.' She said nothing and Don's face hardened. 'Unless he thinks that every acre in the parish is sacred,' he said.

She and Don then began to quarrel between themselves, a silly hissing quarrel conducted in whispers and raised eyebrows. She was entirely on her fiancé's side, but for her uncle's sake she couldn't help protesting that a large-scale development in the area could threaten the Shrine – if only by taking from its dignity.

'Its dignity?' Don gave her a contemptuous look.

'I mean its importance.'

'That's more like it,' Don said, and he turned and went back to his own room, cross now with her as well as with the Canon. Was he only bluffing, she wondered, as she closed the door and went over to the window to stare out into the darkness. Could there be any real possibility that the impoverished earth out there could yield a proper livelihood for the people and free them from the ignominy of selling cheap religious objects to the sick and dying? It was hours before she went to sleep.

And now, this morning, as she lay sipping her tea, Mary looked out again at the bare and desolate land that even by day was dark or else lit fitfully by a harsh, glaring light falling on it in shafts between rain-laden clouds. When she was up and dressed, and as she ran down the stairs to the little parlour, she deliberately forced herself to appear gay and friendly.

The parlour was frightfully hot and stuffy, and the Canon was sitting in his battered armchair reading his Office, in front of a fire which had obviously been burning for several hours. It was roaring up the chimney. Although the door was open, the heat was stifling, and yet the old man had dragged the chair closer to the fire. His dog-eared breviary had been familiar to Mary since she was a child. As always when she appeared, he took up the burnt-out pipe that rested on the arm of his chair and put it between the pages to mark the place. But this morning he did not greet her. Instead he glanced at the delicately constructed glass-and-brass carriage clock that stood to one side of the mantelshelf in a clutter of odds and ends, among which pride of place was shared by a photograph of her mother and a framed photograph of the Shrine.

'I was going to get Ellen to give you a call,' he said. 'We'd want to start soon if we're going to pick up that fellow of yours in time for his lunch.'

Mary's heart lifted. If her uncle was going to fetch Don himself in his own car, he must have made up with him this morning, after all. 'He ought to have had his fill by now of plodding around in the mud,' he said. 'And we don't want the meal to be dried up and not worth eating.'

'Thank you, Uncle,' Mary said, but she glanced at the clock. In doing so she had to put her hand up to shield her face from the heat. The room was positively suffocating, and the smell of roasting meat coming up from the kitchen made it seem hotter still. 'It's a bit early yet to go for him, Uncle,' she said gently, and she sat down on the other side of the fire. 'You've no idea how carried away he gets when he's doing this sort of field work.'

'I can imagine! I can imagine!' the Canon said, but he looked across at her oddly. 'What is the purpose behind this foolish expedition?' he asked. To her relief, she saw by the expression on his face that this was less a question than a sneer. Not prepared to cross swords with him, she thought she'd jolly him into a better humour by taking a bantering tone.

'If anyone has to wait about in the cold, better him than us, Uncle!' she said. 'He never knows when to stop on these forages. He'll be laden down like a pack-horse when we find him, his pockets full of sand and rocks and lumps of clay. Wait till you see!'

Not knowing that the slightly derogatory tone in her voice was intentional, the old man chuckled.

'In that case he might be glad enough to see us arrive ahead of time,' he said drily, but he settled back into his chair. A moment later he looked across at her sharply. 'He wore his good suit, did you know that?' It seems a bit odd he didn't bring a pair of old trousers if he intended grubbing around in the clay.'

'Oh, he probably only took the notion when he got here,' she said cautiously. As far as she could see the Canon was not really suspicious, just sceptical about Don's abilities. He leant forward. 'No matter what you may think to the contrary, my dear, your young man is no different from all the other engineers in Ireland today. From Fair Head to Mizzen Head there isn't an engineer in the country that hasn't had his head turned by the tall stories that are going the rounds about the mining up in the midlands, the sinking of oil wells and all that. They're puffed up to the gills with nonsense. They all think they'll make themselves into millionaires overnight.'

'I don't think you're right there,' Mary said evenly. 'It's only the politicians and the foreign investors that are getting anything out of the mining in Meath. The people who owned the land originally got very little. I understand most of them were bought out early in the game. As for the engineers, they are foreigners for the most part. I can assure you, Uncle, the whole operation didn't bring much prosperity to the local people, unless maybe to the shopkeepers and the common labourers.'

The Canon pressed his lips together. 'I'm glad to hear that at least. I've no sympathy with the Meath people. Why weren't they content with what was to be got off the top of the ground, in God's good sunlight, without burrowing into the bowels of the earth? The land around Trim, Navan, and Kells is the richest land in Ireland. Every blade of grass up there would have been a stalk of pure gold to the poor people down here. People with large families of children at that! Not the withered old bachelors that own all the land up there.

But no! No! The people up in the fat grassland weren't satisfied with God's plenty! They had to try and lay their hands on lazy money, get-rich-quick-money. Mark my words, Mary, those people won't be satisfied until they've turned Ireland into another Lancashire. They won't stop until we have slag heaps as high as Aberfan, where we once had the greenest fields in the world.'

He was so incensed that Mary felt she had better try and calm him down. 'To give them their due, Uncle, I believe the mining companies themselves are making great efforts to preserve the amenities. They remove the topsoil and set it aside with the intention of putting it back after they've sunk the shafts and got the under-ground structure ready for work. The landscape will be completely restored in a few years' time.'

'Is that so?' She couldn't be sure if he believed her or if he was being sarcastic. In any event his eyes had suddenly been drawn, as by a magnet, to the photo-graph of the Shrine and dwelt lovingly on it. 'Thanks to the good God, our little Shrine is bringing more prosperity to the people hereabout with every year that passes. It's not only providing them with their daily bread but giving them spiritual food as well.' Mary could only stare at him in amazement. It was Don's contention, and the start of the quarrel, that the local people were being destroyed by what Don called trading in the Temple. She looked sharply at the old man. He was no fool. He could not have forgotten Don's words. His own words must have had some obscure intent. He stood up. 'What puzzles me, Mary, is why, after the views he expressed last night, your young man should want to subject himself again to a sight apparently as objectionable to him as our blessed grotto.' Did she fancy it, Mary wondered, or was there anger still smouldering behind his eyes? 'What's this his words were?' he asked. '"Commercial exploitation. Trading on the frailty of the sick and infirm."' Mary winced. It was a pity Don had used such strong words. Her uncle had mimicked him to the life. Then, lapsing back into his own voice he uttered one single word. 'Guff!' he said. 'Guff!'

'Oh, Uncle, Don didn't mean you to take things up the way you did!' she cried. 'He was really and truly concerned about the poverty down here. He'd never seen anything like it!'

'Well, why then can't he appreciate the money the Shrine is raking in for these poor people. They are making more money every year. Wait till we implement our plans, and have a new car park and a decent hotel, then you'll see!' he said. 'Tell your young man that, Mary! Make him see it.' It was almost as if he was trying to win her as an ally. 'Do you know, Mary, it's my belief that under cover of pretending to make this survey, or whatever it is he's up to, your young man may have had it in mind to go down to the Shrine again, behind backs as it were, and take another look at it, and maybe revise his opinions in the light of how I presented the facts to him this morning, when he blustered out a lot more of his silly socialist nonsense and tried to be blasé. I'm pretty sure he was only trying to save face, and give himself time to think over my words.'

Mary couldn't believe her ears. How could a man like him – she glanced around the parlour so crowded with books and prints, paintings and maps – how could a man who had devoted a lifetime to study, a man who read in four or five languages, how could he delude himself to this extent? Her uncle, however, was going from strength to strength in his delusion. 'Between ourselves, my dear, we may have converted the fellow! God works in mysterious ways, you know.'

Suddenly Mary became more alert. Was it possible this last idiotic remark was a sly probe.

'Don is not going anywhere near the Shrine, Uncle,' she said assertively. 'Not until he has finished his survey. He's only meeting us there because it's a convenient place to meet, an easy landmark.'

Her uncle merely smiled indulgently. 'Ah, well. One way or another I suppose we may as well humour him. Let him rootle away to his heart's content if it makes him happy. The worst that can happen to him is catch a cold in the head.' He winked at her. 'Not that we'd want him laid up now that he's got his new job.'

Mary would have been only too glad to change the subject and talk about her fiancé's prospects were it not that she was now worried on another score. 'The appointment isn't absolutely certain yet, Uncle,' she said. 'I thought you understood that? That's why we're not putting our engagement in the paper just yet. Of course we'll get married whether he gets the job or not, but things won't be so smooth for us if he doesn't get it.'

'They certainly won't. It's preposterous to think of it.' It was touching to see how concerned he was about her future. 'I thought he was dead certain to get that job? Why didn't you tell me there was doubt about it?

I don't know that I could have done much. If it were
in my own diocese I might have had some influence,
but all the same there's never any knowing what a
few words mightn't do if whispered into the right
ear.' He frowned. 'Is it too late now to make a few
inquiries?'

'Oh yes, I think so, Uncle,' she said, but lightly,
because although there was undoubtedly still a small
uncertainty about the appointment, Don felt fairly
confident of getting it all the same.

'Well remember, you've only to say the word,' said
the Canon, and he winked at her again. Then, looking
away once more, he said an extraordinary thing. 'You're
sure of the other thing? I mean to say I hope he's the
right man for you and all that?'

She was very much annoyed. 'Uncle! How can you
ask such a thing? I wouldn't have brought him all the
way down here to see you if I wasn't certain about
that.'

The old man sighed. 'Don't be cross with me, my
dear. You must know I don't like losing you. Things
will never be the same again when there's somebody
with us all the time.'

Mary jumped up and gave him a light kiss on the
cheek. 'Silly-billy! Don isn't just "somebody". You'll
find he's the most marvellous, marvellous person.
Just because you had a little disagreement with
him –'

That was a mistake.

'Did you say a little disagreement?'

Mary gave him another quick kiss. 'Don't be so
touchy, Uncle.' She looked down at him. He had put
on the scowl by which he used to try to intimidate her

when she was small, but which generally just made her laugh. Remembering those days, she looked at him pertly. 'You've got to like him,' she said, stamping her foot like a child.

The Canon softened. 'Ah well,' he said. 'I've no doubt you'll get your own way in this as in everything else, my dear. I've spoiled you for too long to expect matters to be mended now.'

'People are never spoiled by love, Uncle, and you know that,' Mary said soberly. 'One day you'll love Don just as much as you love me.' Ignoring his raised eyebrows she went on, 'Did I ever tell you he was going to do geology, but his family felt that engineering was more practical?'

'Good for them,' he said. 'They were quite right.'

She was glad to see she'd succeeded in distracting him by this piece of information. 'I'm afraid, Uncle, he wasn't really reconciled to it until he and I began to think of marriage.'

'Don't worry. Engineering is a better bet any day,' said the Canon. 'A county engineer gets a fairly decent salary – and that's the main thing, isn't it?'

'I suppose so,' Mary said, doubtfully. 'All the same, I can't help feeling he's clipping his wings for my sake.' Seeing the scowl come back on his face, she hurried to make her point clear before he interrupted her again. 'I think he'd like to put his gifts to work in some way that would bring him more personal fulfilment.'

'Nonsense!' The Canon positively glared at her. 'Personal fulfilment indeed! What does that mean in the name of God? There's only one form of fulfilment for any man in this, his one and only earthly life, and that is – ' He broke off suddenly and Mary was frightened for a minute by a fiery glint that came into his eyes, until she realized it was only a reflection from the flames, into which he was staring. In any case, a second later he seemed to have forgotten what he had been saying. 'Well, he's young, he'll learn, like the rest of us,' he said. 'But you must be his helpmate, Mary – in this, as in all else. You must be God's voice from now on, speaking quietly but clearly in his ear, day and night.' He fixed her with a fierce gaze. 'That's why I'm not really worried about last night's diatribe against the Shrine. I know when you're married you'll knock sense into him. I'll admit it upset me, at the time, to see you so spineless, but I hope I am able to make allowances.'

In spite of the heat of the fire, Mary, on impulse, knelt down beside him. 'Uncle, you must know, you must have seen, that the views Don expressed were not just his own. You must have realized I share them. If anything, they originated with me.'

To her amazement he didn't seem angered.

'Ah, that's only natural,' he said, and he chuckled. 'The male makes the nest but the female has to lure him into it, so she may sometimes have to change her colours for a short time in the courting season, like the birds and the beasts, but when she finally settles down, she shows her true colours and rules the roost. I have no fears about you. If God sends you children I know you'll bring them up in the way our Holy Mother the Church has ordained.' He nodded his head in agreement with himself. 'I suppose I may take it for granted that this fellow of yours hasn't altogether lost the Faith in spite of his spouting last night?'

'Of course not,' Mary said crisply. 'He goes to Mass and so on, if that's what you mean. Most Sundays anyway.'

But her uncle's face darkened again and he grabbed the sides of the chair as if he found it hard to control himself. 'Mary!' He was outraged. 'Mary! That's no way to speak of Holy Mass.' But his outrage was centred less on her than on Don. 'So he goes "most Sundays"! How condescending! I hope his Maker appreciates his graciousness!'

'Don't worry! I'd say his Maker has more appreciation of him than you have!' Mary said hotly. 'But please let's not quarrel about him, Uncle. No matter what you think of him, surely you're glad he's not taking me out of Ireland altogether, in which case you and I might never see each other again? It looked at one time as if we might have to emigrate.'

With relief, she saw she had struck the right note at last. He was visibly touched.

'I didn't know there was ever any question of that.' The Canon seemed stunned by the mere idea. 'Where would you have gone?' he asked dully.

'Oh, I don't know,' Mary said carelessly. 'Things didn't come to that. I suppose it would probably have been Africa, or somewhere like that.'

'Preposterous!' The Canon's exclamation was as vehement as if their going was still a possibility. He actually shook his fist in the air. 'I can tell you I'd never let that happen. Not without putting up a struggle.' He sat forward. 'Are you sure you're telling me the truth, Mary? Are you sure there's no danger of his being turned down for this job even yet? Perhaps I ought to telephone one or two people – just to be on the safe side. Oh, Mary, Mary,' he cried, and his anxiety now had a pathetic quality: 'Apart from not wanting you to go far away, I couldn't bear to think of you living anywhere else in the world, even after I'm dead, except in our own safe little island – God bless it.'

For the first time since her arrival the evening before something of his old affection for her showed in his eyes, and Mary was saddened when she noticed a scattering of large flaky freckles that she hadn't seen before on the backs of his hands. A sign of age? The big brown blotches were disfiguring on his otherwise fine thin hands, with the fingertips slightly bent back. Wasn't that, too, a sign of something – generosity?

Then, as she was staring at his hands, the Canon raised them and clawed at the arms of his chair, trying to drag it still nearer the fire. When he failed, because of the heavy iron fender that was in the way, he heaved himself forward and held his hands almost on top of the flames. Surely he couldn't be cold? Mary had already pushed her own chair as far back as it would go against the bookcase behind her, and yet she was still uncomfortably hot. But although her uncle's forehead was glistening with sweat, she saw that his bony hands were white and bloodless. She was stabbed with pity for him, and it occurred to her that it was as if face and hands did not belong to the same man, just as this parlour where they sat, with the accumulated treasures of a lifetime, did not seem to belong under the same roof with the bleak bedrooms overhead, furnished with ugly outsized furniture, the relics of former priests of the parish. The Canon's own bedroom was particularly cold and uninviting, and it was always pervaded by a sour odour that made Mary shudder on the few occasions in recent years when she had gone in there to help the old housekeeper turn his lumpy mattress.

The room he had appointed to her, years before, when she'd come on her first visit – it was the Easter holidays – was, then as now, bleak enough too, God knows, but he had allowed her to paste up gaily coloured pictures cut out of magazines, and they partly hid the hideous yellow wallpaper. Now mildew from raindown had worked its way through these glossy pictures, and some of them were peeling off the walls, but Mary's heart melted to think how she had grown to love the dark ugly room. Compared with the clinical bareness of her cubicle in the convent, this room had a power to tug at her heart. Even last night its charm was not quite eclipsed. And no wonder! It was the only real home she'd ever known, because however tightly the Canon clung to the belief that she remembered the home her poor mother had tried to hold together after the death of her husband, Mary had in fact almost forgotten that former existence. She had even forgotten what her mother looked like, but, knowing that her uncle could not bear to think that all memory of his beloved sister had been totally obliterated from her mind, she used to nod in agreement with him when he'd extol the dead woman's hair, her eyes, her classic profile. After all, the photograph on his mantelpiece was always there to vouch for her beauty. Mary looked up at it now, but seeing her look up, the Canon thought she was looking at the clock.

'Is it time to go, do you think?' he asked.

'Let's give him another few minutes,' she said.

'Well, then – ' The Canon went back to his breviary.

Mary smiled. The daily reading of his Office always seemed a heavy burden on him. He certainly seized every odd minute to get it over and done with. It was a wonder he didn't know it by heart. Surely some priests did? While he was reading it, she gave herself up to the quietness that had fallen over the room, broken only by the fall of a coal from the fire. She would let him finish, and after that they'd go and fetch Don.

The old man was a long time reading his Office. Mary may even have dozed off, because she started violently when her uncle placed his breviary on the arm of his chair and stood up. 'Where is your coat?' he asked. His own was always thrown across a chair near the door in case he got an urgent sick call.

'It's on the hall rack, I think,' Mary said, getting to her feet and going towards the door, but there she stopped in surprise and peered into the semi-dark behind it. 'That's not another new painting, Uncle? Not another Jack Yeats?' It was an unnecessary question. There could be no mistaking the glory of colour in sea and sky, and although she hadn't seen it till then, the small painting, once seen, dominated the room. 'How much did you pay for it?' she asked, off guard in her excitement. Yeats's prices had been rising steeply.

The Canon glanced nervously down the hallway before answering, and then, to her amusement, he raised his voice. 'I got it cheap,' he said loudly. 'For nothing!' Then he lowered his voice again. 'It's important, Mary, to keep these things from going out of the country, no matter what one has to pay for them,' he said.

'No excuses needed, Uncle,' Mary said, laughing, but she felt she had blundered badly. 'Why hide it away behind the door though?' she asked after a minute.

The Canon looked at his painting with a mixture of pride and embarrassment. 'It's a good enough place for it when the door is shut,' he said sheepishly.

'And when is this door ever closed?' Mary asked slyly. 'You can never close it because the room is always at oven temperature.'

But looking around the room she saw there was not much room for the painting anywhere on the crowded walls. Nor was it a bad idea to place it at a distance from the two large Yeatses on the opposite wall, particularly since they belonged to the painter's early period. She went closer to the little painting, and for a moment let its beauty stream into her soul. Then she turned teasingly towards the old man. 'I suppose there is no trying to wheedle you into leaving me this in your will?' she asked with mock seriousness. 'I suppose you'll be leaving it to the Church with the rest of your treasures?'

'We'll see. We'll see, my dear,' the Canon said. She saw she had made him very happy by her approval of his purchase. 'Mind your p's and q's and you never know what you might get!'

Uncle and niece smiled into each other's eyes. They were on familiar ground now. This was the kind of playful dialogue that used to give them such fun when she was a small girl. One day she had artlessly disclosed that she thought all his possessions would some day belong to her. 'When you are dead, Uncle, I mean,' she'd added, with a child's idea of tact. But young as she'd been, she was quick-witted enough to stand rebuked by her uncle's answer. He'd gone over to the mantelpiece and taken down the photograph of the Shrine with the church in the background. 'And the Shrine as well?' he'd said. She'd bitten her lip in shame and snuggled against his frowzy soutane to hide her blushes. So now, remembering the sweetness of their relationship in those days, and grateful for all he had done for her, she grew serious.

'Oh, Uncle, you've given me so much! Don't ever think I took it for granted. Thank you. Thank you.'

The Canon too grew serious, even harsh. 'Don't make me regret it, that's all. Let's have no more performances like last night,' he said.

And, believing her promise could be kept, she held out her hand. 'No more, I promise,' she said.

'Come on then,' he said. 'Get your coat and let's be off.'

Before the Shrine was built, and before the new trunk road was constructed, the church was seven miles from the parochial house. This was an unusually long distance between a priest and his church, but in the impoverished countryside there was no nearer place of a standard to accommodate a priest. And at first the Canon had not complained of the long drive, even in the cold of winter. But after the Apparition, and especially after the erection of the grotto on the site where the Blessed Mother and the holy saints had appeared, he changed and now could scarcely hide how sorely it chafed him to be so far from the sanctified spot. One of his long-term plans was to build a new parochial house nearer to the centre of activity. Meanwhile he had to be content with the new road which cut a mile and a half off the distance between him and the Shrine. Now, as they drove off, Mary wondered if he had had a hand in getting the new road built. A word in the right ear? She smiled indulgently at him.

They had only gone a few yards along the new road when they came to the place where the old road ran off it. This old road had had to be left for the convenience of a few cottages which would otherwise have been isolated, but it was not maintained and was in a poor state of repair. Yet, when they came to it, Mary impulsively put her hand on her uncle's sleeve.

'Oh, Uncle, would you mind if we went by the old road?' She was not really clear why she made the suggestion, but it did not seem too preposterous considering that the abandoned road looped back again to rejoin the trunk road a few miles further along. She saw at once from the Canon's face that she'd dampened his spirits, which had been rising steadily since they left the house. He resented anything that would delay the joyful moment when he'd catch his first sight of the church spire. Although disgruntled, he dropped into a lower gear and turned on to the small dirt road, but when after a few minutes the curve brought them around again to face in the direction of the Shrine, his good spirits were restored. It was as if the compass needle of his heart had swung around with the steering wheel. And when the spire of the church eventually appeared Mary knew that he would be the first to see it, not because his eyesight was better than hers, but because it was with the eye of love he'd pick it out.

Love, she thought sadly; it was love that was at the root of all the contradictions in him. He thought he had cut out all need for it from his body, and although for a time his natural feelings for her mother, and later for herself, had seemed to fill the vacancy, it was not enough. The vacuum had to be filled and he had filled it with devotion to the Shrine.

She glanced at him as he strained over the wheel, staring straight in front of him. Of course, she thought, of course his eyes of flesh could not but see the tawdriness and vulgarity of the traders' booths at the entrance to the grotto, but the inner eye of love looked through them to the spot on which he believed the Virgin had appeared, and in time the whole place became transfigured for him. Mary sighed, and she too looked ahead, but she was looking only at the road which was more rutted and riddled with potholes than she'd realized. And when, just then, they came to a bad patch and she joggled against the old man, he started.

'Move over, Mary,' he said sharply. 'You're in the way of the gears.'

Like a scalded cat Mary edged as far over on the seat as she could. She'd forgotten how sensitive he was to being seen in public with her. Even when she was a small girl he was always constrained in her company if they were out anywhere in public. He never, then, permitted himself the simple signs of affection he'd show her when they were at home. On the rare visits he'd made to Dublin he seldom took her out for a meal to a restaurant or hotel. Instead, he'd buy delicacies and bring them to her flat and have her prepare a feast for herself there. He was especially ill at ease whenever she had to travel in the car with him. Broadminded as she hoped she was, Mary had a certain sympathy with his dread of giving rise to scandal. She had seen people looking at them oddly on occasion. Worse still, she had found herself looking with curiosity at other priests she saw in the company of women, although in those cases, too, there was most likely a blood relationship. Sometimes even here in his own parish, where he was well known, she knew he was uneasy in her company, thinking that strangers – visitors to the Shrine for instance – would not know she was his niece. Yes, there was some sense in the old man's scruples. It would be a sorry thing if, having unfailingly honoured his vow all his life, he should be misjudged at any time, but sorrier still if, when he was old, he were thought in the end to have succumbed to lust. Poor dear! Her heart melted and, seeing a pile of booklets on the tray under the dashboard, and taking them for new hymn books, she pulled one out, intending to compliment him on it. When his face lit up she realized with a sinking heart that the booklets were about the Shrine.

'Oh, I forgot to show you those, Mary,' he said. 'Ignore the cover, my dear, it's not meant to be a work of art, you know – it's intended to sell for sixpence, which will barely cover the cost of publication. We'll only break even after we sell three thousand.' His face clouded over, but only for a moment. 'We're hopeful the whole edition may be sold out after next summer's pilgrimage, and we've already planned some important changes in the second edition. Open it, open it,' he prompted as Mary sat apathetically with the booklet unopened on her lap, dazed by the realization that a simple mistake had brought them back to the dangerous topic. 'The print is bad, I know that,' he said. 'And there may be printer's errors in spite of my having read the proofs myself – ' He had slowed down the car in order to see her reaction. 'Go on, look through it! I'd be glad of any criticism you have to make. You can't study it carefully now, I know, but I'll give you a copy to take back with you. I'll give you several copies so you can distribute them among your friends. Your young man might even like to have one – after he's been down at the Shrine for a second time.' Here the old man nudged her, and Mary could hardly suppress a shiver of apprehension. She opened the booklet but immediately her attention was arrested by a line on the first page.

'Oh Uncle! I didn't know the Shrine was not recognized by the Church,' she cried.

'Read on,' the Canon said, complacently. 'There was a misunderstanding at the beginning. That's all. It has been recognized now – more or less.' He paused and cleared his throat, and then to her consternation broke into such a pat defence of the Shrine that she felt he must have recited it so many times that he had it off by heart. 'The Church is, at all times, reluctant to guarantee the authenticity of any apparition – except, of course, those recorded in Holy Scripture – but, after proper investigation, the bishop of any diocese can declare that, as far as human testimony can be relied upon, a given apparition may be said to have taken place – or to have given the appearance of having done so. This declaration does not imply a binding obligation to believe on the part of the faithful, but it is recognized practice to regard such a place as sanctified.' There was an almost hypnotic quality in the old man's voice, but as he neared the end of the peroration he sounded a bit rattled. 'It was a destructive element in this country that put out the story that our Shrine had not been granted full recognition.' He turned accusingly towards her. 'You as a Catholic, Mary, ought to know that there is not such a vast difference between proven authenticity and a pious recommendation to the faithful of such devotions as arise out of custom. Read on. Read on. You'll see that the Holy See was pleased to grant many liturgical privileges to our Shrine.'

Mary no longer needed to be urged to read. She was devouring the cheap print. In spite of having been familiar with the Shrine since she was a child, she was astonished to see how little she knew about the actual Apparition.

'I never knew all this about its being such a wet night, such an awful night – '

'Torrential rain,' the Canon confirmed, nodding his head vigorously. 'You don't mean to say you didn't know that! Now you see the need for my little publication. The parish priest at the time had just come from a sick call and was drying his clothes by the fire.'

'That's such a personal detail it makes the whole story come to life,' Mary said, genuinely amazed. 'Don must read this.'

'Of course he must,' said the Canon. 'It's extraordinary how many people are ignorant of what happened here, although if they'd put their pride in their pockets, and come down here, they'd see that the same glow of sanctity that emanated from those heavenly figures still shines down on us today and on all who come to us.'

Mary was scarcely listening. Indeed she felt obliged to offer an apology, an explanation, for her absorption. 'It's not so much the supernatural aspect that fascinates me, Uncle,' she said, 'it's the ordinariness of it all. Those people who first saw the strange light at the church and thought nothing of it – that's so human, isn't it? And then, the others, who actually saw the figures, but thought they were only statues! Can't you imagine thinking that yourself?' She laughed. Then she stopped laughing. 'Oh, but there's something that doesn't ring true. When they saw that the feet of the statues were not touching the ground they fell down on their knees and started to say the rosary. Yet in the middle of the rosary they jumped up and ran around the town to tell everyone a miracle had taken place, and work up a crowd. Now that was a bit hasty, don't you think? That smacks to me of the fake miracle at Templemore, a bit claptrap – '

'Claptrap?' With a jerk the Canon braked the car and brought it to a standstill. 'You missed the real reason for their conviction,' he said sternly. He leaned across her and leafed through the thin pages. 'They saw that the ground was dry under the feet of the Virgin. You must have missed that, Mary.'

'Yes, I did, but all the same that seems to me to be a bit – ' She hesitated.

' – a bit what?'

'Well, a bit small-minded, Uncle, if you don't mind my saying so, a bit petty in the middle of all the marvels, for the Blessed to keep themselves dry when everyone else must have been soaked to the skin.'

Her uncle looked flustered. 'Well, what would you have had them do, hold umbrellas over their heads – the Virgin, I mean, and the Blessed Saints?'

Mary laughed half-heartedly. 'No. I didn't expect that, but why couldn't they have picked a fine night to appear?' She looked back at the booklet. 'One of those poor people kneeling there in the rain was over seventy. It's almost as bad as if they – the Virgin and the others – *did* have their umbrellas with them!'

'Mary! Watch your words, please. I'm used to irreverence, but blasphemy is another matter.'

'Sorry, Uncle.' Mary patted his knee. 'But you asked for my opinion – about the booklet, I mean,' she added tactfully. 'And something about the way this is put makes it hard, for me anyway, to swallow.'

The Canon started up the car again. 'All miracles are,' he said succinctly.

Mary had to agree with that. 'I suppose so,' she said. Then she gave an exclamation. 'Wait! Here's something I consider downright unedifying. When one family ran out they forgot all about a poor old woman who was dying and whom they were meant to be minding. They left her all alone.'

The Canon gripped the wheel tightly and began to go faster. 'She didn't die, though. Did you see that? That you might say in itself was a kind of miracle within a miracle. The old woman struggled out of her bed and tried to follow them, a woman who was at death's door.'

Mary said nothing to that. What was there to say?

She had to admit to herself that the Church had in general examined the case very thoroughly. On the other hand, the case for authenticity seemed to have at least one weakness, a flaw, in fact.

'It says here that those who testified to having seen the Apparition were afterwards said to have been drunk at the time.'

The Canon, however, seemed to exult in this charge. 'Agreed!' he cried. 'That is an accusation commonly made by enemies of the Church. But I am happy to say it is an accusation that is easy to refute in our case.'

'But one of those who saw the Virgin was a boy of twelve,' Mary cried. 'Another was only five! What need was there to prove those children were not drunk?' She laid down the book and turned and looked steadily at the old man. 'I repeat, Uncle – you asked my opinion and here it is. It seems to me that it's easier to believe in the Apparition than it is to believe in this promotion of it. It's all this promotion that seems fishy, especially years afterwards when the evidence, even at the time, was scanty.' Putting the booklet back where she got it, she made up her mind that Don must not see it. 'As for the Vatican's affiliating the Shrine with the basilicas in Lourdes and Lisieux, and granting facilities for pilgrimages – well, quite frankly – ' She was going to say, irreverently, that this piece of propaganda stuck in her gizzard, but they had come to the place where the old road joined the new, and the Canon was sitting bolt upright, getting ready for his first glimpse of the church spire. He'd only got a vague drift of what she'd just said.

'Lourdes and Lisieux, did you say?' he asked, absently. 'They'll only be in the halfpenny place in five or six years from now. The fame of this place is growing by leaps and bounds, and when the new basilica goes up and we have a car park and public conveniences – ' He stopped. 'The expansion will be such that there won't be a shop site to be had within a three-mile radius. There will be shops stretching out as far as this junction! And they'll all do a good business, too. People may not stop on the way into the town – they're always too eager to reach the Shrine – but on their way out, even when they're anxious to get home, either because of small children being jaded and cross, or because of some poor invalid in the back seat of the car who is dreading a long return journey, you'll find there will still be plenty of people stopping.' He seemed to brood for a minute on what he'd said and then nodded his head emphatically in confirmation of its truth. 'In their eagerness to get to the grotto people often forget to buy a souvenir, a rosary or a crucifix, to take back to some old person, a relative, or a neighbour maybe who was good to them in former times, and although they couldn't be expected to turn around and go back, they mightn't grudge the time it would take to stop at a shop along the route.' He turned earnestly to Mary. 'I don't think it would be asking too much of anyone to hop out of his car and snatch up a scapular or an *agnus dei* if he thought it might solace some poor soul, do you?' Mercifully, Mary was spared from giving an answer because the Canon had caught sight of the spire. 'I see it!' he cried, triumphantly, although it was a few seconds before Mary herself could discern against the dark rain-laden clouds the

slightly less dark steeple. Within a few minutes they
drew up outside the church, standing in its shamble
of wooden stalls, with the enormous granite grotto, so
grotesquely disproportionate to it, at its gable.

The grotto was unusually empty of people for the
time of day. There was no sign of life except for a fat
pigeon pecking at the litter in the gutter.

There was certainly no sign at all of Don.

'I knew he'd keep us waiting,' Mary said, just to
humour her uncle, but as she spoke, the door of
Mullins's shop opened and Mullins ran out in his shirt
sleeves hastily swallowing down the food in his mouth
as if he'd been at table when he spotted them.

'Good day, Canon. Good day, miss,' he gushed.
'Are you looking for the young gentleman?' To Mary's
disgust, he ogled her. 'I recognized him as he was
passing here about an hour ago, and I ran out. He was
glad to see me, and he gave me a message for you,
Canon. He said not to wait your meal for him and that
he'd make his own way back.' Then he turned to Mary.
'He had a message for you too, miss. He told me to
tell you he had hopes – whatever he meant by that!'
The disgusting fellow leered again, having evidently
put some interpretation of his own on what might be
those hopes.

'Thank you,' Mary said coldly.

The Canon was more cordial. 'Good man, good
man!' he said, and without going into the church he
pulled up for a minute at the grotto and looked
appraisingly at it.

'We need more litter containers,' he said, clapping
his hands to shoo away the pigeons. As the Canon
turned the car, Mary saw with some amusement that

there were splatters of bird droppings on the heads of the Blessed. Then as they drove past the open door of the church she saw the red glow of the sanctuary lamp and bowed her head from force of habit. The Canon, however, bent over the steering wheel, was heading out of the place at a speed unusual for him. Mary looked in surprise at his face. It was suffused with a dark red flush. And when he spoke his voice had a savage intensity.

'What was behind that message Mullins gave you?' he demanded. For a moment she thought that having seen Mullins's leer, her uncle, too, had read something ugly into it. Next minute she realized he had read the message rightly. 'So that's it!' he cried. 'I was slow for once in my life.' He brought the car to an abrupt stop. 'Tell me the truth! What tomfoolery is that fellow going on with?'

'Oh, Uncle. Let's not go into it now,' Mary said desperately.

'Explain yourself, miss!' said the Canon, and although his form of address harked back again to her childhood, this time it had, as it was intended to have, an adverse effect on her.

'This is neither the time nor the place to discuss the matter,' she said coldly.

'You're right there. That's certain,' the Canon snapped back. 'And let me tell you this, miss, the right time will never come. Whatever that fool of a fellow may have in mind, he doesn't know that backing is needed for a scheme of any kind, whether it's sound or not. Not only here but in every country in the world. And I can assure you here and now that in Holy Ireland there wouldn't be one solitary soul who'd back up a scheme that would – ' he paused ' – would interfere with a place sanctified by tradition, and hallowed by the presence of so many sick and suffering human beings.'

'But, Uncle,' Mary cried, 'Don doesn't necessarily envisage development of any kind in the immediate vicinity of the grotto.'

'Bah!' said the Canon. 'Didn't I tell you our own enterprise will spread over a radius of three or four miles from the present centre.' His face was now so inflamed by fury that Mary was frightened for him. He was actually shaking his fist at her. 'Do you think if those developers were once given their head there'd be any controlling them? Do you never read a newspaper? The gang that's mining up in the County Meath are planning to re-route the road from Naval to Kells. Did you hear that? You didn't? Well, that shows the lengths they're prepared to go to accommodate their own interests. And there's talk of altering the course of the Boyne, the most historic river in Ireland, or in Europe for that matter. Those fellows wouldn't think twice of shifting a whole town if it got in their way – ' Suddenly, the old man seemed to lose himself in thoughts of his own. 'Heathens and infidels,' he muttered. Then he swung around to face her again. 'It's a pity your fine fiancé didn't take himself off to hell or to Africa or wherever it was you said he was going. A great lob he'd be for the country that would get him.'

Mary was absolutely staggered. She wouldn't stoop to remind him that she would have been going with Don. 'If that's the way you feel about him, Uncle,' she said with as much calm as she could command, 'the best thing I can do for both of you is prevent you from meeting again.' She opened the car door. 'I'll get out here if you don't mind.'

The Canon was greatly taken aback. 'How do you think you'll get back to the parochial house?' he blustered. 'You're not as fit as that footballer of yours.'

If he meant to mend matters by drollery, he was making a big error. 'I'll manage,' Mary said. 'If he should happen to arrive back, perhaps you'd have Ellen ask him to take our car and come to meet me.' Seeing he only partly got her meaning, she looked straight in his face. 'Perhaps I could trouble you to put my overnight case in the back seat.'

'You're not coming into the house at all?' His bluster was gone, but he still didn't believe she was in earnest. 'What about the meal? What about all the trouble Ellen has taken over it?'

'I'm sorry,' Mary said. 'Truly I am. But you must make what excuses you can.'

She got out of the car.

Going back along the trunk road the Canon drove fast, and when he arrived at the parochial house he went straight into the parlour and threw a few logs on the still fiercely burning fire. Then he called down the passage to Ellen.

'I'll be eating alone, Ellen. They had to go back,' he said to her, giving no explanation. He frowned when the old woman pattered up and stood in the doorway with a bewildered look on her face.

'You didn't let them go back without anything to eat, did you?' she asked. 'Not all the way to Dublin?'

'What's that?' The Canon seemed surprised at the mention of Dublin, as if his thoughts were elsewhere.

He recollected himself. 'Yes, to Dublin,' he said, but he smiled enigmatically, and when Ellen sloped away he closed the parlour door. A plan had already formed in his mind and was acting as ballast to keep him steady. All the same, to fortify himself further, after he'd shut the door, he stood still and took a look at his little painting. But with the door closed the lighting on it was wrong, and the glass reflected back the white glare from the window, obliterating the glorious colours. To have had it glassed was a mistake. He shouldn't have listened to the gallery-owner who had insisted that due to its rough texture, the paint would get damaged if it wasn't given protection. He bent and peered into the emerald whorls of the shore grasses and indigo deeps of the sea. He wasn't at all sure that the paint hadn't already been damaged even before the glass was put over it. For that matter, now that he studied it closely, he wasn't sure he approved of Yeats's over-liberal use of the palette knife. That was a fad Yeats got talked into when he was old and sick. He bent closer still and opened the door a fraction to put the painting once more into shadow. Yes. He could see it better now. The heavily laid-on paint in sea, sky, and shore certainly gave dimension to the solitary human figure in the foreground. But the figure itself was not much more than a conglomeration of blobs, swirls, and coagulated lumps of crude paint. The Canon felt that if he stuck his finger into one of those blobs it would burst and turpentine or linseed would ooze out from the canvas. The over-use of the palette knife might yet bring down the prices Yeats was fetching, he mused, turning away in irritation from the picture. It had not calmed him. Stalking into the hall he yelled out once more to Ellen. 'Don't bring in my food till I tell you, I want to make a phone call.' Going back into his den and closing the door, he lifted the telephone receiver and, lowering his voice, gave the operator a name and a number and asked her to put through a personal call.

A few minutes later there was the crackle of a voice at the other end of the line.

'Ah, Tim? Is that you?' said the Canon, his temper enormously improved. 'It is? Good! How are you? Same here! Same here, thank God. Well, look Tim, I won't hold you up with preambles. I'll be seeing you next month anyway at the Priests' Retreat, but look here! Do you happen to recall a fellow who was in the seminary with us, a fellow that cracked up badly and was sent home? Wasn't his name Gargan? Yes, that's the fellow. Yes. Yes, he got over it fairly well and married and reared a family. Yes, yes. I know that. That's right. That's the very fellow. Well, what I wanted to know was whether I'm right in thinking that although the story given out to us in the seminary was that he was being sent home, he was really being sent – as we guessed at the time – to the other place? That's right. That's what I thought. Could you tell me something else, Tim? How long was he in that place? Oh! is that so? You don't say? He must have been a fairly bad case. Anyway, be that as it may, thank you, Tim, for the information, but let me ask you something else before I let you go. Would you say it ran in the family? Ah well, I know all that. Times have changed and so on. Thanks be to God they have good doctors there, now at any rate. They can work wonders with electric shock and insulin. I was listening to a programme about that on the radio only the other day, but I think they still have reservations in some cases. Apparently there are cases where it is what you might call congenital, and then – Yes. Yes? I'm listening. I agree. I agree entirely. That's what I thought. And that's why I'm phoning you. You know, I suppose, there's a job coming up in your diocese – ah, don't worry, Tim, just a run-of-the-mill job – district engineer. There must be hundreds of suitable applicants. Well, I understand the decision is more or less made, and it's being given to a young fellow who – what's that, Tim? Oh!' Here, although he was alone in the parlour, the Canon chuckled. 'Ah, you read me,' he said. 'That's the very man, a son of our other man. Oh, this young fellow – what's that? Yes. Yes, I've met him. Yes I agree he seems to have all his marbles – more than his share would be more like – that's not my objection to him, although it might be thought a district engineer ought to be fairly responsible – cambering roads and building bridges and that kind of thing. By the way, did you read in the papers about that terrible business in America recently, where forty or fifty poor souls went to their death when a bridge collapsed. And hundreds were injured. It was way out in Ohio, or somewhere like that, but people are people the world over. Well, as I was saying, I wouldn't like to be whoever was responsible for appointing the district engineer in that case, would you? I think I'd sooner be one of the poor unfortunates that plunged to their death in the river. I'd even go so far as to say I'd rather be the man that made the miscalculation, than a member of the selection committee that didn't vet the applicants properly. Ah yes, yes. I know that only too well, Tim. All the same, we can't neglect to do our homework, can we, when it comes to matters like this?'

Here, the Canon began to tap his foot impatiently on the linoleum. 'Yes, yes, Tim. I hear you. I know what you're trying to get across to me, but let me ask you another question. Did you ever read a book called *The Bridge of San Luis Rey*? You didn't? Ah, what's the the matter with you? Are you going to seed up there in the fat land? Look, I'll bring it to the retreat and let you have a loan of it. Don't forget to give it back, that's all. There's a powerful description in it of a bridge collapsing. It will interest you, apropos of this matter we're discussing.' Here, however, the Canon seemed to suffer a loss of memory. 'What's this we were talking about anyway?' he asked. 'Oh, yes, about that job – ' There was a brief pause while the Canon listened to the voice at the other end of the line. 'No, that would be far too late. You'll have to act at once,' he said emphatically. Then he put his hand over the mouthpiece of the phone. 'Excuse me a minute, Tim,' he said, and raised his head to listen to the sound of a car starting up outside, followed a few seconds later by the sound of a car driving away. 'Nothing wrong, nothing at all,' he reassured his listener. 'But, with regard to this job, Tim, I know what I'm talking about. There's more to this than meets the eye. There are more reasons than one why we don't want this type of fellow in a key position. Do you get me? You do. Well, I'll see you at the retreat. And I won't forget to bring you that book.'

The Canon's face had resumed a normal expression, and he seemed about to hang up the receiver when there was another crackle on the line. His expression changed slightly. 'Yes, I know he is engaged, which makes it more awkward, I admit. In fact there's something I'm not sure I ought to mention. I think I'd better though, since you'd find out anyway, you old fox! And I hope when I tell you, you'll see how concerned I am for the public good. You see, it's to a relative of my own the fellow's engaged. Yes. Oh, you knew, did you? Well, all I can say is, I'm sure that like myself you must have thought she'd have done better for herself, a pretty girl like her, and clever as well. Diabolically clever, you might say. You might even go so far as to say that in many ways, as God made them, he matched them. But let me make one thing plain. You're not to let yourself be concerned over my niece. I can't afford to be concerned about her myself in a situation so grave. The fellow may be all right – who knows – but that's not to say that we can let him be placed in a position where even the slightest weakness could result in calamity for untold numbers of people. Don't be concerned about Mary, Tim. A bit of experience outside Ireland never hurt anyone, and she's no more of an exception to that rule than he is. Never fear, they'll be back home in a few years, and if he stands up to the test of time we might be able to do something for him then, eh? I may be on the blower to you if that time comes, Tim! We might fix them up with something similar to what they're aspiring to now – if we're both in the land of the living, which I hope, God willing, we will be. By the way, while we're on the subject, I didn't ask about the old lumbago? Ah, good! Good. That's about the way I feel myself.' A thin trickle of laughter came down the wire and was echoed by a loud confident laugh from the Canon. Then apparently he had cause to give his friend further reassurance. 'Oh, stop worrying about the girl, Tim. Women are only interested in making a home. It doesn't matter a damn to them where it is – Dublin or –' He frowned. 'Or Africa, or wherever.' Since the last word seemed a weak one on which to end, or wanting perhaps to give a professional touch to the conversation – the Canon's voice took on an unctuous tone.

'God bless, Tim,' he said.

'God bless,' the answer crackled back. 'God bless.'

Tom

My father's hair was black as the Devil's, and he flew into black, black rages. When he spoke of death, as he often did, he spoke of when he'd be put down in the black hole. You could say that everything about him was black except his red blood, his fierce blue eyes, and the gold spikes of love with which he pierced me to the heart when I was a child.

He had made a late, romantic, but not happy marriage. All the same, he and my mother stayed together their whole lives through. They drew great satisfaction to the end of their days on this earth from having kept faith with each other.

They had met on shipboard – on the S.S. *Franconia*. My father had gone to America when he was young, and was going back to Ireland to buy horses for the man he worked for in East Walpole, Massachusetts. My mother was returning home from a visit to a grand-aunt and grand-uncle in Waltham, where the grand-uncle was pastor of the Roman Catholic church.

My mother's family lived in County Galway. They were not very well off. They were small-town merchants who sold coal, seeds and guano as well as tea, sugar, and spirits. My mother was the eldest of twelve. It used to puzzle me that the eldest of twelve should go visiting in a land to which most Irish men and women in those days went as emigrants. Such a visit suggested refinement, and this was affirmed by her classic beauty, her waist – which was thin as the stem of a flower – her unfailing good taste, and her general manner. My father had set his eye on her the minute he went up the gangplank – she was already settled into her deck chair, reading a book.

They did not marry till three years later, when, after a correspondence conducted more ardently by him than by her, he sent her a diamond ring and money for her passage out again – this time to marry him. They were married from the parochial house in Waltham.

My mother hated living in America, and on three occasions when my father let her go to see her people he had to follow and fetch her home. When she spoke of her ocean crossings, whichever way she was going, my mother referred to them all as visits, until the last one, when, eastward bound and taking me with her, she knew she'd never have to go back. My father had drawn out some of his savings and given her money to buy a house in Ireland. She bought it in Dublin. Then he gave up his job, took the rest of his money out of the bank, and went to Ireland himself – for good.

My father never seemed to feel resentment against my mother for forcing him to return to the land of his birth. He may not have felt any; his savings, although modest, enabled him to cut a great dash in his native land. He had brought home with him a car that looked so large on the narrow Irish roads that when we went for a drive of a Sunday it seemed at every minute as if the sides would be taken off it by the thorny briars in the hedges – hedges so high they made other cars look like cockroaches. Sitting up at the wheel of that car in a big coat with an astrakhan collar was a far cry from running barefoot across country in County Roscommon, where he had been born.

'Why didn't we go back to Roscommon to live?' I asked him one day.

His blue eyes blazed with contempt for my foolishness. 'I have to educate you, don't I?' he said. And I suppose he imagined, like all poor emigrants, that in the place of his birth time would have stood still – the children going barefoot to school, doing their sums on a slate, and mitching every other day, until at last, like him, most of them would run off to England and thence to America with scarcely enough schooling to write their names.

Although my father had a deep and a strong mind, and was the subtlest human being I ever knew, he had had small schooling. He could read and write, but with difficulty. He came, indeed, from stock that had in the penal days produced a famous hedge-schoolmaster, and this he was very proud. It may well have been his pride in this scholarly kinsman that led to his own premature departure from a one-room schoolhouse in Frenchpark. For one day the schoolmaster, in a poetic discourse on spring, invoked the cuckoo, and made reference to the cuckoo's nest. My father's hand flew up, and, without waiting for permission to speak, he gave voice to his shock and indignation. 'The cuckoo doesn't build a nest! She lays her eggs in another bird's nest!'

'Is that so?' The master must have been sorely nettled by this public correction. 'Well, boy, if you think you can teach this class better than me, come up to the blackboard and take my place.' Then, abandoning sarcasm, he roared and caught up his cane. 'I'll teach you not to interrupt me!' he cried.

'You're wrong there, too,' my father said. 'You'll teach me nothing more as long as you live.' And with that he picked up his slate and fired it at the master's head. Fortunately, for once his aim was bad, and he missed. Instead, he put a gash an inch deep in the blackboard, and in the hullabaloo he lit out of the door and down the road for Dublin. He was in such a rage he forgot to say good-bye to his mother, whom he never saw again in this life. He spoke of her to me three or four times, and I'm sure it was of her he was thinking on that occasion, leaning over a gate staring into the deeps of a field in a mood of utter blackness.

From Dublin my father went to Liverpool, from there to the potato fields in Scotland and the hop fields in Yorkshire and, finally, one Palm Sunday morning, he arrived in Boston, then a leading port. All he took with him to America were the memories of the boy he had been, running barefoot over the bogs and the unfenced fields of Roscommon with a homemade fishing rod in his hand, or maybe a catapult. That boy used to think nothing of running across country from Castlerea to Boyle, and even into Sligo. Towns that lay twenty miles apart were no distance to him – leaping stone walls like a young goat, bounding over streams like a hound, and taking the corner off a lake if there was wind to dry out his clothes. Whenever I think of what it is to be young, I find my mind invaded by images of a boy – a boy running over unpeopled land under a sky filled with birds. My father had made his memories mine.

My mother had her memories, too, but she had so

many of them they seemed to take up all the room in her head. She never discarded duplicates. She had a hundred memories of summer evenings when she and her sisters and cousins strolled around the rampart walls that enclosed the small town where she was born. There was the same tinkle of laughter in every one, and the same innocent pretence of surprise when the girls met their beaux taking the air in the same place at the same time. Winter evenings could have been reduced to the tale of one evening in one parlour, my mother at the piano, with her sisters in a half-circle around her singing high and the beaux in an outer ring singing strong and low. I was an only child, and when I was small I liked to think about those gay young people swaying back and forth, their mouths like swinging censers spilling song to right and to left. But I got tired of hearing about them, and in the arrogance of my own youth I thought those memories of my mother's had used up all passion in her. Long before I knew what passion was, I knew there was no passion between my parents. Not that my mother wasn't always telling me proudly about all the American women – that is to say, Irish-American – whose expectations had been dashed to the ground when my father arrived back from Waltham with her as his bride. And she displayed with amusement his bachelor trophies – a topaz tie-pin, a set of silver-backed brushes, and a half-dozen or so pairs of gold cuff-links. He had been the most eligible bachelor in East Walpole, she many times assured me. He was nearly fifty and had never been caught. It was my mother's code that nice girls never tried to catch a man but had themselves to be snared. She herself was thirty before she was snared.

Everyone thought she was much younger, she said,
until the midwife took the opportunity of asking her
age in a cloudy moment just as I was about to emerge
into the world.

'Your father's admirers were all a lot older than
that, though,' she told me. 'They must have been out
in America for years to be able to buy those expensive
presents, because you may be sure they left Ireland
empty-handed.'

My mother's own trunk could not have been very
heavily laden, but she based her estimate of what the
others brought with them on the fact that they had
travelled steerage. She had travelled cabin. My maternal grandfather, as well as wholesaling grain and guano,
was a shipping agent for the Cunard and White Star
Steamship Lines, and my mother knew all about poor
Irish emigrants, no matter what grandeur they later
assumed.

My mother had a state-room to herself, and the
courtesy of a reduced fare arranged by the Queenstown agents of the line. It was her firm conviction that
no one – no woman, that is – could ever live down the
stigma of steerage. Her state-room in cabin class was
a symbol to her of how my father had lifted himself up
by his marriage, he, of course, having gone steerage on
his first crossing. By the time they met on the *Franconia*
he had elevated himself to cabin, else they would not
have met.

'He would never have been happy with any of those
women,' my mother explained to me in East Walpole.
I knew them all by sight. They were plump and jolly,
and usually to be seen in the company of their husbands
– at a ball-game, or watching a parade, or just sitting

side by side with them in matching rocking-chairs on their front porches. My mother never rocked on her porch. She never went to a ball-game. She watched only one parade, and that was when the United States entered the First World War. Then she stood at the gate of our house on Washington Street – then a post road from Boston – to see the American boys marching to camp. She cried all the time, thinking of her brothers back home in Ireland. Mostly she stayed at home, doing embroidery or reading. She didn't believe in tagging after a man everywhere he went.

I had my doubts about the wisdom of this, and once made a sly reference to my father about his former admirers.

He looked at me with astonishment. 'They'd never have given me a daughter like you,' he said. 'You have not got your mother's looks, but you have her ways.' I understood then that my mother's ways were an abiding source of his pride.

Sometimes I wondered if it was my father's lack of education that had kept my mother from marrying him in the three years that followed the voyage on the *Franconia*. He'd asked her as they parted on the quayside at Queenstown, she told me.

'But I took a dislike to him at first sight,' she said. 'I'd noticed him coming on board and I objected to the way he was staring at everyone, especially at me. I wasn't surprised when he came up to us and broke into our conversation.' She had become acquainted in the departure shed with two elderly English gentlemen, who had helped her find a porter to carry her steamer trunk and arranged with the steward to have her chair placed between theirs. They also urged her to choose first sitting, which was the sitting they favoured. Their company was most enjoyable, she maintained; it was they who made the voyage so pleasant. They were both married and spoke very nicely of their wives, who hadn't accompanied them because this was a business trip. They showed her photographs of their wives, and said that their wives, too, had read and greatly enjoyed *The Weaver*, by John Parker, which was the book my mother was reading when my father caught sight of her from the gangplank.

It was in this book, that she'd left on her deck chair while she went down to the dining saloon on the second day out, that my father wrote his name. He scribbled it in the margin of the page at which she'd left it open. And after that, every time she vacated her chair he wrote his name on whatever page was open.

'It was a very cheeky thing to do,' my mother said. 'My sisters would have been horrified.'

Then one day, when she was playing quoits with the nice elderly gentlemen and the one who was partnering her put down the quoit for a minute to rest, my father picked it up and finished the game. Naturally, they won, my father and herself. And after that he partnered her into the finals, and victory. They were presented with a silver rose bowl, which he immediately gave her but which I never saw. It vanished into thin air during the three years that passed between playing quoits on shipboard and playing at marriage on dry land.

The two gentlemen between whose deck chairs my mother's had remained stubbornly placed used to tease her about Tom. 'He'll propose to you before we dock in Queenstown,' one of them prophesied, and the other agreed. They urged her to accept him. 'He's a good man, Nora,' they said.

'But I refused him!' my mother would insist, with a laugh that still rings in my ears. It was a pretty laugh; her face was only a small part of her charm. 'He had a cheek, scribbling in my book.' I think she had suspected from his handwriting his lack of schooling, and it would not be long until his letters proved her right.

I have often wondered what became of his love letters to my mother. What did she do with them? Surely bad spelling and grammar would not be cause for a woman to destroy her love letters? His letters to me, written the times she took me away from him to Ireland, told so much love it lies on the pages still, although the ink has faded and the paper frayed. I have them all treasured away. Among them there is one on pink paper that he wrote me after he'd come back to Ireland to join us. It was written on the eve of the Grand National, and he was going to Liverpool for the night. He had just had time to come to a hockey match in which I was playing left wing, but he hadn't been able to stay for the finish. I should explain that in his day he had been a great athlete – a champion hurley player, but at a time when everyone on the team was expected to score from any place on the field at any time and however he could. He wrote:

Dear Little Daughter,
This is a Pound For Pin Money and I hope ye will win. I was very Much Disopinted how you Plead

you Seem to wait till the Ball Came to you that is
Rong you should Keep Moving and Not to stay
in the One Place. God Luck,

Dadey.

'Dadey' is nothing unusual – just 'Daddy' spelled
his way. I wish he hadn't written 'ye' for 'you' – it
looks like stage Irish. But it also shows that my father
never felt obliged to spell a word in the same way in
the same sentence, much less the same page. It was as
if he felt that he could give new meaning to a word
with each new spelling – or, at least, a different in-
flection of meaning. It was as if for him a letter had a
visual quality and could impart a message beyond its
mere words. How often I saw him, after he had labori-
ously composed a letter, lean back from it the way a
painter might stand back from his easel and, grabbing
up his pen, jab at the page again, dotting an 'i' or
crossing a 't' and adding 't's and 's's or doubling an 'l'
or 'n' at a furious rate, until he felt he had given the
composition a more powerful effect.

His letters to me must have roused at least as much
love as was put into them. I keep them in the velvet-
lidded box where my mother kept the trinkets he
received from other women. In this box I also keep a
few souvenirs that my mother herself seemed to treasure beyond their value: a silver Child of Mary medal,
a gold-plated Communion cross, and a buttonhook of
real but hollow silver. That buttonhook baffled me –
it seemed to emphasize what I thought was the shallow-
ness of her feelings. Why had she kept a thing like
that throughout her life? It had been a casual gift, and
an odd one, from a customer in her father's shop – a

customer whom in her lifetime she always 'Mistered'.
Mr Barrett – that was how she referred to him. It
seemed a distant way to refer to any man.

'But he always called me "Miss Nora"!' she said
when I questioned it.

Mr Barrett was a land agent on a large estate called
Multyfarnham, a few miles outside the town ramparts.
My mother met him one afternoon when she and her
sister were picking the daffodils that grew in rings
under the trees in such numbers they never regarded it
as stealing to pick them.

'When he caught us, Mr Barrett said we were only
thinning them out,' she explained. And she said it was
to make sure she was happy in her conscience that he
called that evening to buy a drink in her father's shop.
'Only a glass of port wine,' she hastened to add. 'He
never drank anything else.' It was clearly a token
drink to make his call acceptable to her family – as if
anything could, it seemed from the tone of her voice.
Why they disapproved I did not at first understand. 'I
used to stay out in the shop talking to him for hours,'
my mother went on. 'My sisters would be furious.
We all played the piano, but I was the best. What made
them mad with me was that I stayed out in the shop
until closing time.'

'Couldn't you bring him into the parlour?' I asked.

'I thought I told you!' my mother cried. 'Mr Barrett
was a Protestant!'

'Oh?' That was all I managed to say, but I looked
with my first real interest at the crescent-shaped scar
on her index finger. It was more than a crescent; it ran
almost the whole way around her finger, like a ring. It

was hard to believe it was not a real ring made of ivory or whalebone that had somehow sunk into her flesh and over which, like grass on a grave, the skin had grown. I don't think it would have been visible at all if her skin had not been the deep olive of a Galway woman's, which tradition credits to the wrecking of the Armada off the coast of Ireland. Even when my mother was an old woman, the texture of her skin was soft and smooth. And then, too, that scar shone bright as the sickle moon.

'I was polishing a glass for his port wine,' she said, 'and when the glass broke in my hand he pulled out his handkerchief and tore it into ribbons to bind up the cut. It was a silk handkerchief with his monogram on it.'

'Do you ever hear from him? Where is he now?'

'He's dead,' she said. 'He was found dead one morning in a little ditch that ran between the road and the woods. He used to take a shortcut over it when he was going home at night. He must have slipped on the plank across it. He fell face downward into the water.' She paused. 'There was only half a foot of water, but he drowned.'

'Was he drunk?' It seemed a natural question, and I didn't think I deserved the look she gave me.

'I told you, he only drank port wine,' she said, 'and never more than one glass.'

'How frightful!' I cried. 'Did you feel awful?'

'I didn't hear a word about it for two years. I didn't hear until the time I came back with you – an infant in my arms – to show you off to my family. It happened only a few days after I left for America to marry your father. I inquired about him the minute I came in the door – I was wondering if he ever called when I had gone.' She looked down at the scar on her finger. 'That's when they told me.' She paused again. 'But no matter what they said I knew he never drank to excess – only the one glass of port wine.'

I never asked my mother about Mr Barrett again, even when my father was dead and she might have been prepared to talk more about him.

My mother lived for twenty years after my father – her due, considering that was the difference in age between them. It was not a fair bargain, however, because he had had her beauty when he could proudly display it but she did not have his support when she needed it most. 'Poor Tom,' she'd say. 'If he only knew that I'd be left so long after him, to fend for myself,' or 'If only Tom could see me now, crippled like this, it would break his heart.' And while he had always spoken of death as being put into the black hole, she always spoke of it as 'joining Tom.' And the implication was that now wherever he was would be home to her. And a place of happiness, too.

She used to speak of him during those twenty years she survived him in much the same way that her sisters and brothers used to speak of him in his lifetime.

'Poor Tom,' she would say. 'He was so good to me.'

'Poor Tom,' *they'd* say. 'He is so good to Nora.'

One day when my mother had been dead for two years, I was paying a duty call on an unmarried aunt who kept house for one of her bachelor brothers. We were sitting in the little parlour that had been the scene in my mother's stories of so much brightness and laughter and song, but the day was dull, and our talk was sad, and we often fell silent. In one of those silences, my aunt picked up the newspaper and was glancing at it idly when she gave an exclamation.

'Listen to this!' she said. 'Yesterday some poor young man was found drowned in a small drain with only a foot of water in it. He was lying face downward. They thought he had drink taken, but from the evidence given at the inquest the coroner decided it was suicide.'

'Where did it happen?' my uncle asked listlessly, and when my aunt said it had happened in another part of the country his interest evaporated. But my aunt was devouring the print. She caught my uncle's arm and shook it violently.

'Suicide!' she repeated. 'Just like Nora's Mr Barrett.'

A hundred questions leaped to my mind, but I was silenced by the look on my uncle's face. 'What are you talking about?' he cried. '"Nora's Mr Barrett" – as you call him – was accidentally drowned. You know that as well as I do. What would Muggie think if she could hear you saying such a thing?' Muggie was the name by which my maternal grandmother had always been called by her grown-up family; it was meant to be an endearing diminutive, but to me it had always seemed more appropriate than they knew. In one way or another, she had smothered most of her children.

Had my mother known the truth about Mr Barrett? I wondered. Had my father? Had that knowledge had anything to do with his rare but terrible drinking bouts, and the less frequent but more terrible depressions that came down over him like a snuffer? I had seen that snuffer quench joy in him at times when he should have been happiest, looking over a gate at his pure-bred horses thudding across pastures flowing rich as rivers. Yet his face would darken, and I'd be sure he was thinking that, even before him, they would be put down in the black hole. Tie-pins and silver brushes, he knew too well, could outlast a million men and a million horses.

I was twenty. I had just finished my first university examination, and while I was waiting for the result my father decided to take me to Roscommon, to the place where he was born. He had taken me to Killarney, with its lakes, and Connemara, too. We had gone together to the Glens of Antrim and the Burren in full flower. But I knew these places were nothing compared to a bog land bathed in the light of his memory, a light he thought had no night and over which he thought no cloud could ever settle.

It was mid afternoon when we reached the town of Boyle and took the road to Frenchpark. What would he feel, I wondered, when he'd see the changes inevitable in the time since he'd last been there?

To my astonishment it did not bother him at all that where there had been golden thatch there were grey slates, where there had been ploughshares there were tractors. He hardly seemed to notice that the boys wore boots and not one girl had a waterfall of hair. His eager eyes fell short of these changes and fastened on unchanged mounds of earth, on unchangeable stone walls, and on streams that still ran over the same mossy stones. 'Look at that!' he would cry, stopping the car one place after another and pointing out with delight something familiar. 'Look at that five-bar gate! Many's the time I vaulted it. Look! Look! By God, that's the same old bank I put Dockery's ass over,

digging my toes into its sides like it was into butter I
was digging them!'

Then his eyes fell on something so exciting he could
hardly speak. 'I didn't believe it'd be still standing. By
all that's holy! It's the old schoolhouse!' he cried. 'God
be with the master! I wonder if he's still alive.'

The little schoolhouse was no longer used as a
school, of course. We had passed a large new school a
mile or so back down the road. But Tom got out and
stood staring at it. At last, he went over and tried the
door. It was locked. He looked up, then, at the windows, which were very high up so the scholars of those
days couldn't be distracted by looking out.

'I bet the mark of that slate is still on that blackboard,'
he said, and suddenly he lifted me up as he used to
when I was a child in Boston lifted up to see a parade.
'Can you see anything?' he cried.

'Only cardboard boxes piled up everywhere.' The
classroom was evidently used as a storage place for
the jotters and copybooks, erasers and pencils that
had replaced the old slates and slate pencils of his
day.

He set me down. 'But I'd guarantee the mark is still
on that blackboard!' he said. He gave a laugh. 'If I
thought the master was hereabout, I'd call and let
him see you.' His eyes travelled over the countryside
again. 'There were eighty-four scholars in that little
schoolhouse,' he said. 'And I could name every one
of them.' As if I didn't know! I myself could sing
out that litany of names: Micky Dockery, Tom Forde,
James Neary, Ethel Scally, Mary Morrisroe, Paddy
Shannon . . .

'Most of them went to America,' my father said,

'and I met many a one of them out there. I'd be in a bar
and it crowded, and suddenly I'd see a face, and I'd
know it at once for a Roscommon face. You wouldn't
have to give me a minute till I'd put a name to the face
as well. I'd leave my drink and I'd go over and I'd
slap the fellow on the back and I'd call him by his
name. But if he saw me coming he'd beat me to it. "By
the hokey – it's not you, Tom?" And after that it
would be round for round as long as either of us had a
dollar in our pocket. And it wasn't only the fellows
but the girls. I was with your mother and you one day
in Boston sitting in Childs Restaurant, and I caught
sight of one waitress that was shapelier than the rest,
with red hair that could make you think the evening
sun was on it. "Stop staring, Tom!" your mother said.
She was easy embarrassed. But although the girl had
her back turned to us I could have laid a five-dollar
bill she was from the County Roscommon. "Wait till
she turns around," I said, "and I'll give you her name
into the bargain." But when she turned round she beat
me at my own game. "Tom!" she screamed, and she
left down the tray she was carrying and ran over to us
and began shaking hands with your mother and taking
you in her arms and throwing you up in the air. And
everybody in the place gaping. With all the commotion,
it wasn't long till the manageress arrived on the scene,
but seeing it was Molly Starky she turned away and
let on to notice nothing. Molly wasn't the kind of girl
any boss would attempt to put down. She'd have
pulled off her apron and lit out of the place if anyone
ventured to say a word to her. A real Roscommon
woman! Do you know what happened when we'd
finished eating and I asked for the check? She went

over to the cash register and ran up a zero. "On the house," she said. That'll show you what she was like!' My father laughed.

He looked around him again over the flat land, where, among the new cement houses, there were still a few mud-wall cabins. But there was more grass growing out of their thatch than could be seen in the little fields around them. They, too, would soon turn back into the clay from which they were made. 'She lived over there,' he said, pointing to a cabin behind one of the new cottages. It seemed now to be a cow byre. He sighed. 'But that was a long time ago. I don't know if she's alive at all. There can't be many of the old folk left. There must be a lot of them laid to rest in – ' He paused, and I waited for the familiar phrase about the black hole, but the memories of boyhood were too strong.

'In Cloonshanvil cemetery,' he said quietly, pointing to where in the distance I could see a small, walled cemetery, dotted with marking stones not much different from the rough field stones that surrounded the little plot.

'Is that where your parents are buried?' I asked, thinking of his mother, to whom he had never said good-bye. I thought he'd want to visit the grave.

But he shrugged. 'They're put down somewhere there,' he said, with what I took at first to be a strange indifference. 'I sent money back to the priest one time and asked him to put a tombstone over them, but he returned it and said no one could find the exact spot.' A dark shadow fell over us both for a minute.

'It's a wonder he didn't keep the money to say Masses for their souls,' I said, and at that the shadow lifted and a smile broke like sunlight over my father's face.

'I never thought of that,' he said. 'Ah, but the priests that were going in those days weren't like the priests today. He was a gentleman even if he was a priest.'

We were walking back to the car when we saw an old man coming towards us on the road.

'Let's have a word with this old-timer,' he said, 'and see if there's anyone left around here that I knew in my young days.' The old man was so bent and was walking so slow that we got back into the car and moved forward to meet him. As we got nearer, my father took his hand off the wheel and nudged me. 'He's making his way to Cloonshanvil to save people the trouble of carting him there,' he said.

Yet when we drew level with him the old fellow looked spry enough for his age. His face was weathered by wind and rain, but he seemed as hardy as a wild duck. It wasn't poverty that had bent him double, either; he had a suit of good frieze cloth on his back and a pair of good strong shoes on his feet. As the car stopped, he came over to us with a courtesy not common today.

'Good day, sir.'

'Good day to you, sir,' my father replied, but I saw that he was staring at the old fellow with a puzzled look on his face.

'It's a nice fine day, sir, isn't it, thanks be to God,' said the old man. And, as my father had said nothing, he looked appraisingly at the car. 'That's a fine car you've got there, sir,' he said. 'I suppose it's visitors to this country you are? Is it wanting to know the way to Dublin you are, sir?'

At that my father gave a laugh. 'No,' he said. 'I know this part of the country well enough. I wish I had a dollar for every time I walked this road!' he cried with a jaunty note in his voice.

'Ah, I knew you were from America, sir,' the old man said. 'Sure, Americans have plenty of money for travelling the world and going anywhere they like.' Then he frowned, as if he, too, were puzzled by something.

My father hesitated for a second, and to my astonishment he turned the key in the ignition and put the car into gear. But just before we drove away he leaned out. 'Did you ever hear tell of a young fellow called Danny Kelly?' he asked.

'Is it Danny Kelly? Usen't us two to sit on the one form beyond in the old schoolhouse!'

'Is he still in these parts?' my father asked slowly.

The old man gave a dry chuckle. 'He is!' he said. 'He went to Scotland for a while, but his family brought him back here a while ago. And he'll never be leaving again.' With a jerk of his thumb, he pointed toward the Cloonshanvil cemetery. 'The Lord have mercy on him.'

'The Lord have mercy on him,' my father repeated, and both of them took off their hats. 'There was another young fellow by the name of Egan,' my father said then. 'Did you know him?'

'It would be a queer thing if I didn't! I'm called Pat Egan,' said the old man, but now his blue eyes filled with mild inquiry. 'If it's not an impertinence to ask, sir, where did you hear my name?'

Now, I thought. This is the moment. But my father was letting in the clutch.

'There was a fellow I knew in Boston that came from here,' he said. 'He told me if ever I passed this way to inquire about a few of the scholars that were in that schoolhouse there with him.' He nodded at the little school.

'And what was that man's name, sir, if you'll pardon my asking?'

My father seemed to expect the question, he was so ready for it. 'I declare to God I knew him as well as I know myself,' he said, 'but at this moment I can't recall his name.'

Pat Egan was satisfied. He laughed. 'Wait till you are my age, sir,' he said, 'and you'll be forgetting your own!'

We drove away.

'What do you make of that?' my father asked. 'Pat Egan and me are the same age to within a day. I didn't know him from Adam when we drew up beside him. But when we were a minute or two talking I knew him by a bit of a blood mark that you maybe didn't see at all, because it was under his left ear. But I remembered it, because the female teacher, when she'd be expecting a baby – which was every year – used to make him keep his cap on in class, pulled down well over his ears so she wouldn't see it and it maybe bring bad luck on the child in her womb. I knew him by that blood mark. But he didn't know me from Adam!'

'Why didn't you tell him who you were?' I asked, looking back at the figure of the old man getting smaller and smaller behind us.

'I don't know,' my father said quietly, and then, to

my surprise, he abruptly swung the car into a narrow lane on our left. 'There used to be a cottage up this lane,' he said, 'and many's the time I was in it. I near wore the seat off my pants sitting on an old settle that stood by the hearth. Rose Magarry was her name,' he said. 'She was my first sweetheart.' And now with every word he was giving light little laughs like a stream frolicking over stones. He was so lighthearted I thought I could tease him.

'Oh, you must have been a right boyo in those days,' I said.

He turned angrily. 'What makes you say that?'

'I was thinking about those tie-pins and cuff-links you got from admirers. That's all.'

'Is it them things?' he scoffed. 'A few dollars is all that kind of thing cost in those days. Gold was cheap in America then. The girls could earn as much as us men then. And some were earning more! They gave presents like that to every fellow they met.'

He had slowed down the car and was looking from side to side of the lane. 'We ought to have come on the cottage before now,' he complained.

We were passing a mound of dung that looked like rotted thatch, and among the nettles and elderberry bushes there were foxgloves and hollyhocks, twined together with honeysuckle, and a white rosebush gone wild. Hundreds of bees were buzzing over it, and white butterflies dancing. 'Do you think there might have been a cottage there at one time?' I said cautiously, because I was thinking that if it is true, as legend tells us, that nettles grow out of the bones of monks and men of combat, perhaps honeysuckle and roses grow from the bones of young maidens.

My father was looking where I'd pointed. 'You're right. That would be the spot. I knew I couldn't be so far out in my calculations. The old people would be dead, and she'd be married and gone. Come to think of it,' he said, 'I heard she was married and a widow into the bargain.' He looked ahead, to where there were four or five new cottages, the ground around them as bare as a hen run. 'We'll stop at one of those cottages and ask if anyone can tell us where Rose lives now,' he said. He winked at me. 'Just for fun.'

We stopped in front of the first of the cottages, at the back of which a young woman was hanging out wet clothes. She turned and stared at us, more aggressive than curious. But an old woman, who had been sitting inside the window, got up and came hobbling out.

As she came down the cement path, my father called to her, 'I'm sorry to bother you, ma'am, but I wonder could you tell me anything about a girl by the name of Rose Magarry used to live in that cottage back there.' He nodded back at the mound of rotted thatch and flowers.

The old woman had a touching simplicity. 'Magarry was my own name, sir,' she said. 'Would you be meaning me? I am called Rose. I married Ned Malone, but he's dead these twenty years.'

I looked anxiously at my father. He was gripping the steering wheel and staring straight in front of him. 'I was only wanting to ask because of a young lad that used to know her long ago,' he said stiffly. 'A fellow I met in America. He asked me to call.'

'And what would his name be, sir?' the old woman asked, and it broke my heart to hear the deferential note in her voice. But next minute she threw up her hands. 'Ah!' she said softly. 'Don't I know who that was! Tom! It's his son you are, sir, isn't it?' She darted close and peered into my father's face. 'Tom's son. Sure, you're the dead spit of him!' Then, stretching out her hands, she caught at his and went as if to drag him out of the car. 'How is he? Tell me, is he still alive? But wait, what am I thinking about, you'll come inside and be telling me over a cup of tea? And you too, miss?' she said, recalling my presence. But next minute she glanced back uneasily at the young woman who was all the time standing by the clothes-line staring.

'You'll have to excuse us, ma'am!' said my father. 'We've a long journey ahead of us yet.'

There was a strange little silence.

'Ah well in that case, sir!' the old woman said then, and she seemed relieved. 'But wait a minute, sir,' she cried. 'I'll open the two sides of the gate, so you can turn your car in comfort.'

I waited till we'd turned and driven down the narrow lane and were back on the road. 'Why didn't you tell her?'

He said nothing for a long time. 'Why do you think?' he said, and the black mood that came down on him didn't lift till we'd crossed the Shannon.

The Mug of Water

Esmay didn't mind the portal dolmens. They were great, really. When the honeymoon was over and they went back to London she, too, would be talking about them for weeks. Besides, Denis didn't expect her to go inside. In most cases, anyway, the portal slabs had slipped and blocked the entry. Denis himself sometimes managed to squeeze between the standing-stones and on those occasions Esmay got a grim humour out of hearing him shout to her in his excitement, assuming she'd be pressed up against the stones trying to see all she could from outside. No fear! She kept well back from those gigantic boulders. She didn't like the tilt of the capstones, even though the stones had remained in position for centuries.

They had just seen a very fine dolmen and, as they were walking back to the car and even though her legs had been stung by nettles, Esmay was enjoying the early morning sunshine. But when they got to the car and Denis consulted the maps and booklets the professor had loaded on them, her heart sank to see that the next item on the itinerary was a passage grave. Not another one! It was the passage graves that terrified her. And Denis did expect her to go inside and crawl around in the dark until she was suffocating with fright. No matter how many millennia those great mounds of clay and rock had remained in place, she could not rid herself of a ridiculous fear that they might take that exact moment in time to collapse.

It was their eighth day in Ireland and their seventh in County Mayo, and Denis had got her up bright and early so they'd have plenty of time to see everything. And now they were driving along a low road looking out over the narrow fields that lay between them and the sea. Esmay's heart lifted when yet another inlet gave a glimpse of the dazzling Atlantic crashing against the black, rocky shore.

The view was magnificent. Mayo must be one of the most beautiful counties in Ireland. In spite of the antiquities, she was not sorry it was here they had come. Neither she nor Denis wanted a tourist-type honeymoon. They had had no plans beyond getting to Dublin and hiring a car. And so, when they met up with the professor on the plane and heard his proposal, she raised no objection at all to their going to Mayo for a few days. Indeed, she was happy to see how the professor had fired Denis with enthusiasm, and made him as excited as a boy. They had got into conversation across the aisle in the plane, and Esmay, who had the window seat, had caught only snatches of their conversation – she was deadly tired after the wedding reception – but she heard enough to know that Denis was hooked. And the moment he told her about the spectacular finds the archaeologist had made, she guessed they'd be off to Mayo to see them.

The professor had discovered the site of a prehistoric farm under ten feet of bog, and whereas up until then all that was known of the men of prehistory had been learned from their funerary rites, it would now be possible apparently to find out something about their life habits.

Listening to the professor, Denis was almost oblivious of her until they were flying in over Dublin.

'Esmay! Did you hear that?' he said, and he tried to put her in the picture. He was madly excited and barely coherent.

'I heard,' she said.

'Oh, but you didn't hear what the professor has just suggested – that we go down to Mayo and see the find for ourselves! He's prepared to show us over the site himself and explain things to us.'

'How marvellous!' Esmay was genuinely pleased, mostly because she knew how much Denis would enjoy the expedition. 'We'll go, won't we?' she said enthusiastically enough, not realizing then that they would spend their whole honeymoon burrowing underground like rabbits. Nor did she know that Denis intended to head straight off for Mayo the minute they arrived at the airport. She realized this only when she heard him asking the car-hire people how many miles it was to Westport, and whether they could make it before dark. 'Surely we're not going tonight, Denis?' she cried.

He turned to her in such surprise she was more amused than annoyed.

'Esmay! You don't seem to realize how privileged we've been by this invitation. The news of the find has not yet been released to the press. It won't be released until they have excavated further and catalogued what they uncover. The professor was on his way back after a quick trip to London for special microscopic lenses. They're going to set up a field laboratory down there.' Here Denis frowned. He was already as engrossed as if he were himself professionally involved. 'They'll have a problem when they do finally leak the news. They'll have to devise some system of protection. Irreparable damage could be done by newsmen and photographers tramping all over the place. When the story breaks there will be people coming from everywhere under the sun.' He frowned again – this time at Esmay. 'I don't think you have the faintest glimmer of the importance of Professor Merrit's find.'

'Merrit? Was that his name?' Esmay asked absently. It was nice to see Denis so happy but, after all, a honeymoon was a honeymoon, and this was their wedding night. 'Tell me, Denis,' she said drily, 'when is Professor Merrit himself going down?'

Denis immediately saw the absurdity of his excessive enthusiasm. Not caring who was looking, he grabbed her to him and kissed her.

They did not go down to Mayo that evening. They spent the night in Dublin at the Shelbourne Hotel. And when, once during the night, they woke up, it was Esmay who, to please him, suggested they ought perhaps to start off straight after breakfast. As she looked out of the window she saw that even at that early hour the sky was whitening. It was her first experience of the magical half-light of an Irish dawn. 'Oh, look at that sky, Denis,' she said, but Denis was dead to the world again, intent, no doubt, on conserving his energies for the long drive ahead.

They slept late that morning and lay in happily for a while, but Esmay saw to it that they left Dublin before noon. She knew how much it would mean to

Denis to be one of the first on the scene at Ballyconlon. It would be a feather in his cap when they'd got back to London. She could picture him telling the other doctors about it in the Common Room, or in a slack moment when they were going round the wards.

They set out in top form. Ireland was divine and when they finally reached Ballyconlon, Professor Merrit spotted them getting out of the car and came across a field and out through a stile to meet them. When she learned that the professor had, in fact, gone down the previous night after all, Esmay looked uneasily at Denis, but he was so eager to get to the site that he gave her only a mildly reproachful glance as he trotted off after the professor across a field which, like the surrounding countryside, was mainly bog land.

Before they reached the site Professor Merrit briefly repeated – recapping for her sake – what he had told Denis on the plane. Esmay hardly bothered to listen, knowing that Denis would relay it all to her later.

The site, when they came to it, seemed like any other stretch of bog, except that it was railed off and that the cuttings in it were more precise than those made by the turf-cutters they had seen at work in other bogs. And it was, of course, odd to see a stone wall under instead of over the ground. Otherwise, the wall of loose, round fieldstones was identical with the walls made by present-day man which ran all over the countryside, not just here, but in the west of Ireland generally. To herself, and to herself only, Esmay confessed that she was disappointed. There was so little to see. She tried hard to concentrate on what the professor was telling them.

'It was when we came on this wall alignment, ten feet below the surface of the bog, that we knew we had found a field – a prehistoric field – and that with a bit of luck we might even find signs of the habitations of the people who worked those fields.' Dramatically, he flung out a hand towards where the distant Atlantic lapped the land. 'We already knew that the people who built the tumuli, or passage graves, had beached on those shores three thousand years before Christ, or thereabouts, and we had estimated that there must have been about three thousand people in that particular expedition. What we could not quite figure out was why they had come to this barren and desolate part of the land. But the moment we stumbled on those fields and found evidence of tillage, we knew that the land here must, in that millennium, have been infinitely richer and more fertile than it is today. And when we make soil tests and examine some of the pollen that we were fortunate enough to retrieve, we expect it will prove that the land you see around you may well once have been the most fertile land in the then-known world. There were various types of pollen, and we hope to be able to tell the different kinds of grain that were grown by these prehistoric people.' The professor's face was alight with passion for his work, and his voice heightened as he turned to Esmay. 'They were our forbears,' he said, movingly, and his enthusiasm was infectious. Esmay's own interest quickened and when, rather brusquely, the professor motioned them to move nearer to the brink of the cutting, she almost fell into it in her excitement. Denis had to warn her to take it easy. But her imagination had run away with her, and when she looked down into the freshly cut trench she was bitterly disappointed. There was absolutely nothing to be seen. At least, she could make nothing out of what she saw. The professor, however, pointed out that the soil at the bottom was a different colour from the soil in an ordinary cutting. He explained that they were looking at a ridge system very similar to that of our own day. He said he knew this because the soil between the places where the ridges had been was harder and more impacted than the rest which was, in fact, flattened furrows.

Esmay stared down and tried hard to see what she was supposed to see. To no avail. She glanced at Denis, but was disheartened to see that he was scribbling notes on a cigarette packet. She looked down into the trench again. What had she expected, she wondered. Was it to see a soft, green meadow stirring in the breeze, or golden ears of corn swaying under the weight of their own ripeness. She really was a fool. She was as simple-minded as the ancient navigators who, looking down through the glassy fathoms of ocean, thought to see the spires and domes of lost Atlantis, with its candles and torches still alight in the depths of its watery grave.

Here Esmay made an effort to concentrate on what the professor was saying. If she could not work up as much enthusiasm as Denis, she could at least pay homage to the devotion of those who, like the professor, seemed able to extract so much information from so little material. And Ballyconlon was certainly a beautiful spot.

After showing them over Ballyconlon, the professor himself conducted them across the fields to a neighbouring site, where a colleague of his had made another and only slightly less important find. Then, suggesting other places of archaeological interest which they might profitably visit, he took leave of them. Esmay made no demur at the time, because it seemed only natural that they should take advantage of the opportunity offered to investigate a world up until then almost unknown to them. And the weather was perfect. She and Denis were both agreed on stopping in Westport to get a list of the available farmhouse accommodations, because although they certainly were not counting the cost of their trip, they knew that in the farmhouses they'd get good wholesome food and be brought into contact with simple, ordinary life in Ireland. They were right. If the big double beds were lumpy, it hardly mattered when they themselves were so idiotically happy cuddled up in them together. Indeed, at the beginning Esmay felt it did not matter what way they spent the day-time – but now it looked as if their whole honeymoon was turning into one big archaeological binge. And she was not prepared to put up with that!

Denis had put the car in first gear, and they were creeping along at a snail's pace so he could look from side to side, making sure he did not miss anything, when Esmay herself suddenly spotted a cairn. She glanced at Denis. Smart as he was, he'd missed it. She snuggled down in her seat and smiled secretly. And when the hateful mound was out of sight around a bend in the road, her smile broadened. She felt absolutely no guilt. If anything, the small deception made her love for him more real, as if she had been his wife for a long time and could therefore be excused a small subterfuge because of a good motive behind it.

Denis had stopped the car though.

'I wonder are we on the right road, Esmay? We ought to have come on another cairn to our left, a very important one.' He dived his hand into the glove box and consulted one of the maps. 'This one is going to be excavated shortly. They expect to make a lot of finds.' As he read, he shaded his eyes from the glare of the sunlight. 'Just imagine, Esmay, as late as eighteen-fifty there were over a thousand tumuli in this part of the country alone.' He put the book back and clapped the glove box shut. 'Vandals!' he said fiercely, and Esmay knew his anger was not confined to the Viking marauders but included all hikers and holiday trippers who despoiled these sacred places, as well as local farmers who, until recently, had quarried gravel from the mounds. He was so earnest she nearly laughed openly at him. He shook his head. 'Esmay, I am ashamed of my nationality,' he said. And at that she did laugh outright. Unlike her – she was English through and through – he was of Irish parentage, but, like her, he had been born in London. This was the first time he'd been to Ireland, which made his outburst a little absurd. She said nothing, however, because looking at him she had to admit that after one week in Ireland the Irishness in him had come to the fore.

'Oh, you are a dear, Denis,' she said. She did love him. So much! All the same, she was not able to bite back a facetious remark about the tombs. 'Cheer up, old boy. There are seven hundred cairns still intact.' Privately at that moment she herself felt grateful to all despoilers, historic or otherwise, who had been responsible for diminishing the number of those scary cists in the bowels of the earth. But she was sorry to see she had pained Denis by her lack of ardour. She'd have to be more careful, particularly since he, like a little boy, was probably convinced he'd make a find of his own in one of those old caves. It had not passed unnoticed by her that he had dirt under his nails after he crawled out from some of those holes in the ground, and she'd guessed that he must have been scratching around surreptitiously, hoping to unearth something: a shard, a flinthead, a bead, or a splinter of bone, anything, anything at all, missed out by the experts.

How she wished he would find something, even the tiniest bead, even a bead that wasn't very old at all, as long as he thought it was and as long as it looked it; because although he would talk of getting it authenticated, she'd make certain he did nothing of the sort, and gradually he would come to believe in its authenticity. She wouldn't listen to any talk of their handing their find over to a museum, either. Most museums were too full of junk already. No! They'd hang on to it, and back home, when they had people in for drinks, Denis could pass that bead around and it would give him an opening for telling their guests about the trip. Esmay looked at him again sideways, a stealthy look. He was so boyish, in spite of being a fully-fledged medical man, and suddenly an altogether new force ran into her love for him, swelling it the way a tributary can swell a small river into a mighty torrent. That new force was pity, and she was chastened to think how marriage had revealed to her – to both of them perhaps – small weaknesses that, quite simply, had to come to light if they were to make their way safely through a lifetime together. They certainly would not have survived long on the idolatrous feeling she'd had for him up to their wedding day.

From the first moment she'd met him, she'd been ridiculously sensitive about her own lack of a university education. She'd gone through a really bad time meeting his friends, who were mostly medical students. And his mother had not hidden her misgivings in those early days. She had been shockingly outspoken about the shortcomings of Esmay's upbringing.

'You really have a good mind, Esmay, it's a shame it was not trained,' she said, just as if a mind was like a voice, Esmay thought, making no reply. Denis's mother was an economist, with a string of letters after her name, and she had an important job in the city. 'Why don't you do a degree even now, Esmay?' she said. 'I see no reason why you shouldn't.'

Thinking the older woman might be hoping by this suggestion to postpone the marriage, Esmay had given her a cold smile. But that was not the older woman's intention. 'You might consider it, dear, while Denis is doing his internship. To occupy you. He won't have much time for you then, poor pet, and you could hardly employ yourself more usefully. As well as that, it would ensure that you wouldn't feel at a disadvantage with him later on in your lives.'

Esmay knew her eyes must have opened as wide as windows. It was all she could do not to blurt out what her own mother had thought of Denis's education.

Her mother was appalled the first night she'd been told about him. 'Do you mean to say he's not even a doctor? Just a student?' And even when it was explained to her that he was sitting for his finals in a few months and had expectations of getting a first place –

expectations which were to be amply fulfilled – even then, she still seemed to regard poor Denis as socially half-baked. She nearly had a fit when she heard they were looking for a flat. 'A flat? A doctor can't live in a flat. You'll have to have a house, Esmay!'

'In Harley Street, I suppose!' Esmay was provoked into this cheap retort. 'Mother! You know very well that even after his internship he'll have to get his fellowship and perhaps a registrarship before setting up in practice anywhere.'

Here, however, her mother had shown her mettle.

'No matter! You have to live somewhere. Why not Harley Street?' she snapped. 'With property prices rising you might not be able to get a house there in a few years' time.' Then, smiling, she gave Esmay a conciliatory kiss. 'My dear, your fiancé is at least fortunate in that he'll have a wife properly equipped to further him in his career. Most of the big men of his profession, here in London anyway, owe their positions entirely to their wives. It is their wives who have made them.' Here her mother gave her another kiss – this time a conspiratorial one. 'You must be discreet, though, darling. We must lead them, you know, not drive them.' She spoke as if Esmay were already a married woman, and almost immediately she was off at a gallop with her own plans for the furtherance of her son-in-law's career. She seemed to think that successful doctors had to be hatched out by their womenfolk in the same way as barristers and stockbrokers. There was immense calculation behind the lunches and dinner parties she'd indefatigably given for them after the official announcement of their engagement. And, indeed, at the very first dinner party Esmay was forced to recognize that her mother's poise and sophistication had thrown into sharp contrast what even Esmay herself could see was a certain slovenliness of mind in Denis. No. No. That was not fair. He was only sloppy when it came to social chit-chat. The victim of his own brilliance, he had specialized too soon – going straight from public school to medical school without a proper grounding in general knowledge, and with no travel whatever. By contrast, her own education – at St Leonard's and afterwards at Les Oiseaux in Paris – had shown up rather well. The nuns in both places used to boast, justifiably, that their pupils could and invariably did, take their places in society not merely as the wives of prominent men, but also in their own right. Girls from St Leonard's had become surgeons, directors of companies, even judges and members of Parliament. And one had become a cabinet minister.

But to return to that first dinner party. The conversation had at one point centred on a recent earthquake in Managua, and the guests were discussing oceanic depths and variations of temperature which made certain areas of the earth more liable than others to subterraneous disturbance. Someone murmured that in regard to its geographical situation, England was lucky.

'Although, mind you,' Denis broke in with his usual impetuosity, 'there are tremors felt here in England from time to time. They are too infinitesimal to be normally perceptible, but they are recorded on those yokes in the observatories.'

Yokes?

Startled looks passed from face to face around the

table, and Esmay herself blushed. In spite of his professional veneer, the more remarkable for being premature, Denis could be as slap-happy with words as any paddy. None of her mother's guests was familiar with the ubiquitous word yoke, which the Irish use like an algebraic sign to stand for anything under the sun when they are too lazy to find the exact word. Esmay had to admire the way her mother came deftly to the rescue.

'Those seismographs are really incredibly sensitive instruments, aren't they?' she said, and the guests relaxed at once. That evening Esmay saw what her mother meant about a wife's upbringing being an asset to a husband, and it was not long before Denis too had his eyes opened as to how much better stocked with general knowledge her mind was than his.

But here Esmay was recalled to the present, because the car gave a lurch. Denis had worked out from the map that he had passed the cairn. He was turning the car and going back.

'Ah, there it is,' he exclaimed with great satisfaction as they came in sight of the mound again. 'Isn't it a wonderful day?' he said as they got out of the car, and feeling the warm earth under her feet and looking up at the blue sky, Esmay was ready to agree wholeheartedly, until she realized that he was referring not to the weather but to the good time they were supposed to be having.

Climbing over an iron gate they started up the lower slopes of the mound, and soon the gentle grass gave way to wiry short-stemmed rushes, and heather that put a spring into their step. When they stopped to draw breath, as they were several times forced to do, Esmay looked back over her shoulder at the wonderful view that stretched out wider and wider below them as they wound upward. At last they reached a really steep slope, and the stiffest part of the climb began. In places she had to grub her way along, catching at clumps of heather and pulling herself up by her hands. The sod was now more spongy, and there were wet patches where their feet sank and where Esmay's shoes let in water. It did seem odd to her that it was the low land that was dry and the high ground wet, but she didn't say anything. She really didn't mind. It was only going into the tumuli she minded. And now the cairn was no longer an insignificant nipple on the breast of the hill, it was revealed to be a formidable mass of stones and the entrance to the tomb a terrifyingly narrow one. The massive portal slabs that slanted fractionally made her shudder, although she knew the slant was a deliberate device on the part of the men of prehistory. She remembered that Professor Merrit had insisted that those prehistoric people were very scientifically minded. As she scrambled over the last stony patch of ground, she imagined she could already feel the chill breath that would exhale from the opening, and it reminded her of a time when she'd gone to visit a school friend in Berkshire, and the girl's brother had taken her into the woods the night before a hunt to stop the foxholes. There was this same smell of earth – of death. She shuddered again, this time violently, but Denis did not notice.

'Denis?' She pulled him back. 'Do we need to go inside?' she pleaded. 'It will be just the same as all the others.'

'But, Esmay! This is the one that has the drawings in it.'

As if she cared! He must have guessed by her expression how reluctant she was, because he frowned.

'Those boulders have stayed in place for thousands of years,' he said reprovingly.

'Not everywhere! Didn't you see the concrete buttresses in the last one?'

'A precaution – that's all,' he said impatiently. He must have assumed then that he had overcome her fears, and decided to consolidate his victory by a small display of chivalry. 'Here, let me go first,' he said.

Esmay could have hit him. If she were to be persuaded, once again, to go into one of those awful places, there would be no question as to who would go first.

'What is the point of going into every single one?' she repeated.

'But the drawings? Don't you want to see them?'

'Oh, I suppose so,' she said wearily. 'Come on then.' She must have sounded very graceless because Denis, who had already bent his head and was about to bolt into the tomb, turned with a pained look.

'But aren't you – '

'Of course. I'm having a great time,' she said hastily, and it was true enough. Who wouldn't enjoy this glorious weather and this beautiful scenery? She was interested in the antiquities, too, up to a point. 'I'm terribly interested. I wouldn't have missed it for anything. We've learned so much. It's just that you're so thorough, Denis. I would have thought it quite enough to go into one of these places – just to get the atmosphere. Even Professor Merrit said the photographs and the replicas in the museum in Dublin are – '

'Photographs! Replicas!' Denis turned away in contempt, but she persisted with her argument.

'The detail is enlarged almost to life size, Denis, and there are spotlights focused on them. You can see things you'd never see – ' Frustrated, she didn't finish but caught at another argument. 'Do you know that in Dublin they have the actual bones or bowls or whatever it was they found in these tombs.' The 'whatever' was a mistake, though. It made Denis wince. 'Well, after all, we are amateurs,' she said, but that only made matters worse.

'Speak for yourself, Esmay,' Denis said sharply. 'I was just thinking a minute ago that if I were free to choose another profession I'd choose archaeology.'

That was really going too far. He was being quite ridiculous.

'Well, why not do it now?' she said flippantly. 'After all, you told me last night that you'd only begun to live when we – '

She stopped, realizing that what they whispered at night in the dark might in the daylight be regarded as silly, even in bad taste. She was relieved to see he was not disgusted. Indeed, her words seemed to awaken a belated concern for her.

'Perhaps you're tired, Esmay. It was a stiff climb. Perhaps you'd like to sit down for a few minutes before we go inside?' She noticed he himself was a bit puffed. 'How about a cigarette?' he said, and, picking a sunny spot, he sat down. She sat down, too, but shook her head when he offered her a cigarette. In a way she'd sooner have gone into the cairn and got it over with. Still, it was nice to be sitting in the sun even though Denis had taken the leaflets and maps out of his pocket and was consulting them again. It seemed odd to Esmay that he hadn't been able to memorize what was after all rather elementary information.

'What do you want to know?' she asked. But he wasn't listening. He had taken out his pen and was making more notes on the cigarette packet. He was probably tied for life to the methods of work that had led to his success, putting everything into capsule form and making use of all manner of mnemonics to fasten facts in his mind. Her voice, however, had roused him sufficiently to make him realize they had been sitting down long enough. With a happy smile he got to his feet and prepared to plunge into the bowels of the earth.

'Have you got the candle? And the matches?' she called after him, as his rump disappeared into the opening.

'Damn. Damn.' She heard his curses from deep within. He'd left the candles in the car. 'I have matches though,' he called back, rattling the matchbox to reassure her.

'Are you certain you have enough?' The matches seemed to rattle around too freely for a full box.

'Plenty. Come on, Esmay.' His voice was already fainter, and echoing eerily. With a sigh of resignation Esmay bent her head and went in after him, instinctively crushing her arms to her sides to make herself smaller, and to avoid touching the damp walls. Suddenly she stopped. Why were they damp? Behind her a thin stream of light from the outside world made it possible to see moisture glistening on the stones. It could be a residue of rain, blown in during the night, although she didn't remember it raining. Rain could also explain a livid green fern that sprouted between the stones. Deciding to continue, she lunged forward too quickly and grazed her head. Her body now completely blocked out the light from behind and she was in total darkness. Esmay remembered how the professor had warned them to keep their hands free to feel their way, in case they came on sepal stones, which, he explained, were sharp stones set irregularly along the passage to make it difficult for invaders to rush in and surprise those within when, off guard, they were engaged in their funerary rites. Such nonsense! Esmay allowed herself to doubt the professor's deduction. As if it would be possible for anyone bent double to rush through this passage! The position she had to assume in the cramped passage was one of the things she resented. She felt vulnerable – like a sacrificial victim about to be axed.

This last thought was enough to unnerve her altogether, but since it was virtually impossible to turn around in so narrow a tunnel, she was compelled to go on. She was only consoled by the realization that in here, farther from the entrance, the stones seemed dry. Her throat was certainly dry! Then suddenly, horribly, her fingers brushed against something on the wall, something that moved. If her throat had not been so parched she would have screamed, before realizing it was only another of those ferns. A moment later, infinitely more frightened than before, she stopped dead. How could a living plant flourish in here without air and moisture? Wouldn't the presence of damp suggest crevices, crevices that let through trickles of water, perhaps even a filter of soil? How else could a seed take root? And wouldn't that mean – ? With the utmost vividness, Esmay suddenly imagined she heard a crack, faint at first, then swelling to a deafening rumble, announcing an avalanche of stones and earth that, after thousands and thousands of years, had at last begun their momentous slide. She felt herself getting weak. She would be crushed like an ant in the great collapse, her skull broken open like an egg. Then, oh thank God, away ahead, she saw a yellow spurt of flame. Denis must have gained the central chamber and lit a match. If she could get to him at least they'd be annihilated together. She began to creep forward, when she heard Denis crawling back to meet her. Catching her hand, he drew her safely into the central chamber.

In the beehive cell she was at least able to stand erect. This was such a relief she managed to give Denis back an answering smile before another match, which he had lit, went out. The box really did sound half empty now.

Like all the other cairns they'd explored, this burial chamber, too, was circular, with lesser chambers opening off it, conforming to a roughly cruciform plan, and roofed simply by corbelled slabs. That the great mass of earth overhead could be held up solely by unmortared stones was something Esmay knew she had to take on trust, and she averted her eyes from the roof and fastened them on Denis instead. He was lighting yet another match, and before the flame had properly caught he was peering about.

'Hold it the other way, Denis, for God's sake! With

the head up, I mean!' she cried. 'Otherwise it will burn out too quickly.' But Denis was engrossed in what the flicker had revealed. He paid no heed.

'Look, Esmay. The drawings!'

He was mistaken though. What he took for the work of crude but human hands was only a curious veining in the rock. Like looking for pictures in the flames of a fire, or in the clouds, it would have been easy to delude oneself that these marks were naïve representations of – well, of anything! But the next minute, to her left, half hidden in shadows cast by her own bulk, Esmay herself saw a few scratches that, although simple, looked deliberate. These, she felt sure, were the prehistoric drawings, although they were more like the matchstick figures a child would draw than the work of a man, however primitive.

'There they are! That's a ship, isn't it? And that's what the leaflets told us to look out for – a ship.' Denis was sceptical. Then, peering closer, he agreed that it was a ship. He even gave Esmay a glance of appreciation.

'Now aren't you glad you came in? Professor Merrit said these drawings show the extreme sophistication of early man.'

Esmay wanted to tell him to come off it! But she let his absurdity pass so as not to delay their exit.

'Well, now we've seen them, let's get out of here, shall we?' she said.

Denis, however, was lighting what must surely this time be the last of their precious matches. By its faltering glow he was peering into one of the side chambers, in the centre of which there was the usual large, shallowly scooped stone basin or bowl. The basin was darkened by the shadow cast by Denis's hand as he held the match higher, and he mistook the shadow for a stain.

'You can see where it's blackened by charring. That's were they burned their dead,' he whispered.

Esmay didn't feel like arguing, but she recalled that the professor had said that the dead were probably left out on the hillside until the bodies were decomposed, and then burned, or else perhaps burned outside and only the bones and ashes brought in here. On the other hand, she had read somewhere – in a magazine article at the dentist's perhaps – that in certain megalithic tombs, in Cornwall or Brittany, rudimentary flues had been found going up from burial chambers, which would seem to indicate. . . . She stared in disgust at the stone basin.

But Denis plucked her by the sleeve.

'It was certainly sophisticated of them to cremate the remains of their dead,' he said.

'Oh, don't be ridiculous, Denis,' she said impatiently. 'Cremation is an idiotic word for the hugger-mugger that went on in here. It's a far cry from this place to a modern crematorium.' She really despised his gullibility. 'It makes me sick to hear such creatures called human at all, creatures who burned their dead – ' She fumbled for a forceful word – 'in the raw!'

It was absolutely disgusting to think about what went on in here, no matter how many millennia ago. It was nauseating to think of human flesh, or even human bones, being burned anywhere, much less in this airless cavity. Even when they were displayed in the brightly lit glass cases of a museum, the sight of charred bones upset her – yes, even when they were clearly not human bones at all, but bones of huge animals, thighs or jawbones with the teeth still in them. She peered around. She'd like to know for sure if these prehistoric people really did burn their dead in here. What about the smell? She no sooner thought of that, than she fancied she could get a faint whiff of it still in spite of the immense time span. That nauseating reek! Once, picking a chicken wing by the fire, and being too lazy to stand up and return it to her plate, she'd thrown it into the flames and been punished by a smell that went through the whole house and hung in the air for days, making everyone feel sick. Singed hair was sickening too. As for the smell of burned flesh! Esmay's mind was invaded by that worst of all smells. A few days before her wedding, her mother had persuaded her to have a small and hardly noticeable wart removed from her ring finger. She had had it removed by electrical surgery. But oh, the stench of seared flesh. It made her stomach turn. Thinking of it now, and fearing she was going to retch, she clapped a hand over her mouth and looked around hysterically, hating to have Denis see her vomit. Just then, the last match in Denis's hand gave an unexpected spurt, a splutter that warned it was going to gutter out. And when, to try and prolong its life, Denis cupped his hands around it, his hands cast huge, clumsy, doubled-over shadows on the wall.

Esmay's nerves were stretched so taut that those shadows suddenly assumed the shape of a creature, a thing, more ape than man, crouching over the urn and appearing to gesture and gibber soundlessly. She'd seen an ape in the zoo squatting like that one day, crudely exhibiting its parts, the inner flesh raw and chafed and repelling. That was the way those ape-men would have crouched, crotch exposed.

'Oh, God, Denis! I can't stand any more of this!' she cried, and she groped towards the passage where, although it seemed a million miles away, an insubstantial ray of daylight nevertheless reassured her that it was no longer the terrible half-lit dawn of history, but the day-time of their own enlightened era. Not caring about sepal stones or any other obstacle, she made out of the place as fast as she could.

She was out. Out in the sun again. Oh, God, how good it was! Good to feel the fresh air lave her face. Good to be blinded by light. Good to be back on the surface of the earth that hummed with insects, under a sky criss-crossed with birds. Taking a deep breath, Esmay moved away from the mouth of the tomb and sat down on a hump of wiry grass. With the same refreshing rush as the air over her face, the words of Professor Merrit came back to her, and only then did she fully realize the significance of his discovery. The living habits instead of the dead rituals. The face of the earth instead of its bowels.

Gratefully, she drank in the beauty around her, looking down towards the bay below where, beyond the brown bog, a sheen of light lay on the gentle heaving water as if a shoal of herring had flicked to the surface and were basking there.

Out here on the hillside it was easier to think of those prehistoric people as her progenitors. Out here where, like herself, they would have stood erect.

It was easier now to think of them as human, sailing into the bay below, darkening it with their black bark boats and hailing the land with great shouts when at last it struck into sight. She could picture the oarsmen, their faces gleaming with sweat, rubbing their blistered palms to ease the pain of their long grip on the oars. And the women? She'd forgotten that there would have been women too, but now she could picture them in the bottom of the boats bending over their infants and young children, and wrapping coverings around them as spray licked over the sides. They must have known terror and dismay on the high seas, but the sight of land would have dispelled their fear and their hearts would have leapt up as the prow leapt up with the turning wave and carried them ever nearer and nearer to the shore.

How immense their relief must have been when they beached at last on the white sand and ran up the shingle, their perilous journey behind them. Yet, Esmay felt confused. Were these people the same creatures who had tunnelled the passage graves and burned their dead in stone basins? Depressed, she slumped down with her chin in her hands. Why hadn't she paid more heed to the professor? She lacked concentration, that was it. That was always her trouble, that was where a university training would have benefited her. It would have given her the persistence she lacked in her sporadic bouts of interest in things, and the ability to follow them up by study and research.

Denis was consistently keen. Esmay felt ashamed, now, to think she'd been critical of him. She should have been proud of his lighting all those matches, utterly regardless of having only half a boxful, and peering into every crack and cranny. But what was keeping him? She thought he would have followed her out. He was ages inside. Her heart began to race.

All her old fears and a swarm of new ones settled on her like blowflies. She sprang up and ran to the opening.

'Denis?' she screamed, and without waiting for an answer she screamed again. 'Denis, what's keeping you? What's the matter? Are you all right? Oh, Denis, for God's sake come out.'

There was no answer.

Esmay put her hands to her head, which seemed about to burst. What would she do? She looked around the lonely hillside. Earlier she'd thought she heard a spade striking on a stone as if somewhere near by men were cutting turf. And some distance below she thought she saw a plume of smoke. Before she'd met Denis, or rather before she'd become his wife, a native practicality would have made her act immediately and run for help. But now, after only one week of marriage, she was reduced to total dependence. All she could do was go down on her knees and scream into the dark again.

'Hey? Do you want to split my eardrums?' As he emerged, Denis blinked with the suddenness of his rebirth into the light.

'Oh, Denis!' She sobbed with relief at the sight of him, but she knew she must not irritate him by letting him see she had been scared. Quickly she veered the wind of her words. 'It's so nice out here in the sun. I hated you to miss it,' she lied. 'Do you know what I was thinking while I was waiting for you?' She pointed down towards the sea. 'I was thinking about those people landing here thousands of years ago and all of a sudden, it seemed to me that they were –' She pulled herself up just in time before she'd said that they seemed human – 'they seemed so real to me,' she substituted.

Then her relief at his safety was so great it wasn't enough to see him. She had to touch him. 'Oh, Denis.' She caught his hands and pressed them against her. 'Oh, Denis, I do love you,' she sobbed. His surprise showed her what she'd given away, but she only laughed. 'So much, I mean,' she added quickly, and indeed it was only at that moment she'd found out how very, very much she loved him.

'I should hope so,' Denis said, and she could see he took her avowal pretty calmly. He even moved away a little from her, as if implying that there was a time and a place for everything. To ingratiate herself with him she deliberately referred again to prehistoric man.

'Isn't it sad to think of them so poorly equipped to cope with life. Even out here on this hill, Denis – not like us now in the sunlight but later in the day with evening coming on, or with maybe a storm brewing up – they must so often have been terrified. Like children. Think of when there was thunder or lightning! Even a torrent of rain!'

'I suppose they were childlike in some things,' Denis agreed reluctantly, 'but only insomuch as they must have been curious about the unknown. Curious is the word I'd use rather than terrified. They'd want to find out what it was all about, I dare say.' He frowned. 'Don't forget, Esmay, that it is to them we owe the beginnings of our own knowledge.'

'That's true.' Esmay looked admiringly at him. That, she supposed, was the way he himself, at the start of his career, must have forced himself to look at corpses, to dissect them and put them into jars of brine, and later take them out and handle them. He must have had to tell himself, continually, that he was finding out things that would help others coming after him. Then her misgivings returned. 'But, Denis, even if we accept that they were curious, they must have been frightened, too. When you think that there are people today who are afraid of thunder. There are even people who are afraid in the dark. Oh, Denis, do you want to know what I believe? I believe man hasn't got as far since then as he'd like to think!'

She'd annoyed him again though.

'It sounds odd to me, Esmay, that you should make such a pronouncement in this particular decade, when we've orbited the globe, set foot on the moon and are about to – '

But now she, too, was annoyed. He was wilfully misunderstanding her.

'Look here, Denis. Don't try to tell me those astronauts weren't scared stiff, cooped up in that capsule.'

At this, however, Denis got quite belligerent.

'You seem to forget the astronauts were conditioned for their job. Their training was designed to eradicate fear.'

'Oh yes, I know,' she sneered. 'Breathing exercises! Special diets. But being unafraid to die, physically I mean, does not necessarily mean they were not afraid of death – in the abstract, as it were.' She was not explaining herself very well, she knew, but she felt that if she could make her meaning clear he'd see there was something in what she was saying. 'You may be sure that apart from a fear of death they must have had other fears, worse ones, that nothing short of cutting out their hearts could have eradicated, fears for their

wives and their children and for what would happen
to them if they didn't get back and . . .' Her voice
trailed off, and she made a vague gesture. Seeing that
he was not making any attempt to understand what
she was driving at, she snapped at him. 'You know
very well what I'm trying to say. The more subtle
and complicated we become, the more we get sealed
off from one another.' She was so angry she stamped
her foot.

But Denis caught her hand.

'Oh, Esmay, you are the limit!' he said, and to her
surprise she saw in his eyes the delight in her that a
week ago she had expected always to see, but which,
since they'd come to Ireland, he had lavished mostly
on old stones and mounds of earth. And while she was
looking into his eyes, his delight began to change into
desire. Not here, she thought. Not now! Hadn't he
himself said there was a time and a place for everything?
What about that sound of a spade she'd heard, the
smoke she'd seen? There could be people watching
them, although they themselves could see no one. She
pulled away from him.

'Let's not stay up here any longer. Let's go back to
the farmhouse,' she said. Without standing up,
because the slope was fairly steep, she began to slither
down the heather, careful all the same to watch out for
concealed rocks, sharp as razor blades, that could rip
her thigh.

But it was fun. It was like being on a sled in the snow.
'Come on, Denis,' she called back.

Denis got to his feet all right but he did not follow
her. He didn't move from the spot where she'd left
him. He was pressing the heather with his foot. It was

springy as well as slippery, and with a sudden laugh
he gave a jump into the air, and when he landed he was
catapulted upward again as if he were on a trampoline.
He jumped again. And again. That was the way, when
she and her brother were small they used to jump up
and down on the old-fashioned spring mattresses of
their beds. Gathering momentum with every jump,
they were in the end propelled upward effortlessly and
only fell prone when they were exhausted.

Some day, she thought, laying a hand involuntarily
on her flat stomach, I may have a son with the same
look on his face that Denis has at this minute. This
thought did nothing to allay the longing to touch him
that had returned, and was consuming her with burning urgency. She couldn't throw herself on him, not
up here anyway, but she could at least go closer to him
and give him a hug. She got up to run back, but as she
did so she felt under her own feet – although the
heather looked dry and lifeless – the movement in it.
Like the movement of life in the womb, she thought,
of which admittedly she knew nothing, but which
must be the most wonderful thing in the world. Then
she remembered something else the professor had
said that she had not fully taken in – that the bog was
a living thing, always growing, always in motion, just
like the sea which was not sterile either, in spite of
what its vast briny wastes seemed to suggest. As she
thought of the sea, a strange excitement took possession of Esmay and she felt like throwing herself down
on the heather, knowing that, like the sea, it would
bear her up and sustain her.

'Watch, Denis!' she cried out exultantly, and
extending her arms to either side as if they were wings,

she let herself fall backward. As she knew it would, the heather bore her up, cradled her and rocked her, and, flat on her back with her eyes open, she lay for a moment looking up into the blue sky. The next moment Denis's shadow came on top of her, darkening everything as he stood between her and the sun. All at once, overcome by self-consciousness, Esmay felt foolish, and under her the heather no longer seemed like the sea, but like a bed. Embarrassed, she closed her eyes, and knowing how painfully desire could needle him, she closed not only her eyes but her legs. She made her whole body rigid, cold, and uninviting.

Was he looking at her at all though? Opening her eyes again she half sat up. He was looking at her, but with a deadly white face and a tight drawn expression. What was the matter?

'Esmay!' He was stern as a stranger. 'Esmay, you shouldn't do things like that. There could have been a rock under the heather. You could have struck your head on it. You could have fractured your skull.' At the thought, he winced. She herself only laughed and scrambled to her feet. 'Oh, Esmay, you are a silly ass,' he said when she wrapped her arms around him. 'Don't laugh!' he admonished, although he, too, was laughing now. 'Never, never do that again!'

His concern made her contrite. 'Have another cigarette, Denis, before we start to go down. I'll have one with you,' she said, and she sat down. The sun was directly overhead and the air was warm. 'I'm so happy,' she exclaimed, for no reason, and she lay back. When he threw himself down beside her, face forward on the grass, she caught his hand, but his hand was hot and she was glad when overhead the song of a lark rained down on them, clean and cool. 'Listen.' She sat up. The song tinkled in the clear air, but the lark could not be seen. 'They nest in the ground, of course,' she said meditatively. 'Isn't that odd, Denis, when they are such ethereal creatures? Now that I come to think of it, I've never actually seen a lark. Have you?' She laughed. 'You'd think that they had no bodies, wouldn't you – that they were only notes of music!' Dazzled by looking up into the sun she could scarcely see her husband when she lowered her eyes, but her tongue ran on. 'Some sea birds sleep in the air – on the wing – did you know that? I think it's when they're flying over the ocean.'

Denis rolled over on his side. 'Tell me something, Esmay. How do you know that?' he asked. His scrutiny of her was almost clinical. 'You come out with the most extraordinary things. You seem to know all sorts of things I know nothing about – things I never heard in my life.'

'Oh, just odds and ends,' she said, 'bits and pieces of information picked up God knows where!'

She was glad to see she'd struck exactly the right note. He was pleased with her explanation. Yet he was not completely satisfied. She'd have to explain further. 'I suppose it's because I wasn't at university and my mind wasn't filled up with – ' She was going to say 'junk' but stopped in time – 'with heaps and heaps of technicalities. What I'm trying to say,' she said more slowly and carefully, 'is that my education – I suppose – left parts of my mind vacant, and that is why there is room for all those snippets of information about larks and sea birds.' She saw she had at last made her point. Satisfied, Denis nodded his head and with his hand – and he had large hands – he roughly, quite roughly really, tousled her hair.

'If you ask me,' he said, 'I'd say everything you ever heard must have stuck in that little head of yours.' Then abruptly he looked at his watch. 'I think we might have time, if we hurry, to go to Ballymagibbon. There's a very important cairn there.' Taking out the cigarette packet on which he had made notes, he consulted them. 'One hundred feet in diameter,' he read. Then he put the notes away and took out his map. 'Isn't it odd to think, Esmay, that no Paleolithic remains have come to light in Ireland?'

Esmay smiled. He was at it again. Still thinking he might be the one to make a breakthrough! He was really ambitious this time, she thought. And why not? He might stumble on something. She could even scratch around a bit herself to encourage him.

'After all, archaeology is not a very exact science, is it?' she asked, speaking her thoughts. 'Isn't it mainly guesswork?' Denis looked at her so disapprovingly that she hastily corrected herself. 'I mean that it relies a lot on intuition, doesn't it? Like Newton and the apple.'

'Esmay!' She felt it was all he could do not to call her a fool to her face. Her eyes filled with tears. After all she'd put up with in the last eight days! Climbing hills. Falling into bogholes. To say nothing of having to creep into those awful holes in the ground when, as he knew quite well, she was terrified out of her life. On top of all that it was just too much to be rebuked.

The truth was she had had enough. And she might as well let him see it. You'd think that he, a doctor, would have had more than enough of death without this busman's holiday in tombs and burial chambers. Esmay pressed her lips together tightly. She was not only sick of death and bones, she was sick of Denis! Her heart seemed all at once to have grown cold as a stone. The funny thing was that she'd evidently misunderstood him. He hadn't meant to rebuke her at all. On the contrary! 'Do you know, Esmay,' he said, 'I don't think my mother's suggestion was as foolish as you seemed to think. About your doing a degree, I mean. Even now. It might be a good idea, unless of course – '

'Unless what?' she asked, her voice still rather cold. Then, suddenly, she knew what he'd been going to say, and why he had stopped in embarrassment.

'Well,' she said, slowly and guardedly, 'even in that case, there would always be time afterwards, when our children were reared.' She looked at him mischievously. 'I take it you are not planning on having a prehistoric-sized family?' But her heart had begun to race again and, although she risked leaning over and giving him a kiss, she made it a quick one because the look of desire had appeared on his face again, and she was determined not to start anything – not up here. After one quick caress, she sprang to her feet and was about to begin the descent again – on her feet this time – when he jumped up and, pulling her to him, encircled her with his arm. The lark in the air gave another clear trill.

'Oh, Denis,' she cried, 'wouldn't it be dreadful if we stepped on a nest?'

'Of wasps?' Bewildered, he let her go.

'No. Larks,' she said. Why wasps? she wondered. He was right though. They could just as easily step on a wasps' nest. She stared at him, alarmed. 'They'd swarm all over us,' she said. 'The poison from so many stings could kill a person in a few seconds. It's the same with jellyfish. If you swam into a shoal of jellyfish – '

But Denis threw up his eyes to heaven. 'Larks, bees, and now jellyfish! What *is* this all about, Esmay?'

'I don't know,' she said limply. She was getting confused. 'I didn't say anything about bees, Denis,' she said desperately, but she had no sooner thought of bees than she went off on a new tangent. 'If we found a bees' nest we might be able to steal the honey. Bog honey is black like treacle.'

Fortunately, just at that moment, buzzing over the heather bells, and right beside Denis's ankle, she saw a bumble-bee. It came to rest on a dome of a purple clover. 'There's a bee now! Mind would it sting you, Denis,' she warned urgently.

'That fellow is too busy to sting anybody,' Denis said. 'Look at him!' He pointed delightedly at the bee as it dug itself in between the petals to suck out the sweetness from the stamens, giving short forceful kicks with its back legs as it burrowed deeper. 'Isn't he a sexy little devil,' Denis said, grabbing Esmay to him again so tightly he nearly squeezed the life out of her. Just as swiftly, he released her. 'Let's get back to the farmhouse, Esmay,' he said, his voice thick.

Yes, oh yes, her heart cried, but as they were about to run down the hill she stopped, because of something so ludicrous she hardly dared tell him.

'Oh, Denis,' she cried, pulling back from him. 'I'm so thirsty. I'll have to get a drink of water.' Knowing how unlikely it would be to find fresh water in this boggy place, she could have wept. 'I'm sorry, Denis.'

He was looking at her incredulously. 'Thirsty?' he repeated. 'You're thirsty? Surely you can wait till we get down to the road?'

She wanted to say she could wait – that she would – but the mere thought of waiting made her thirst more violent: her throat was throbbing.

'As we were coming up here, I thought I saw a stream running down against us,' she said desperately. 'Listen! We ought to be able to hear it.'

Denis listened.

'I think I do hear a trickle of water,' he said, and taking her hand he led her across the heather to where, indeed, only a few yards from them, a stream cut through the bog, swift but silent except when it met a rock and leapt over it with a sound like human laughter. 'You have nothing to drink from,' he said. But, laughing, Esmay threw herself down and leaned over the lip of the bank. She was about to scoop up the water in the palms of her hands, when Denis gave a yell. 'Hey! Stop! Hold it, Esmay,' he cried, and looking up she saw that higher up the stream a cow on the bank had let drop a pad of soft, yellow dung that immediately ran down into the water. Disgusted, and almost in tears, she got up.

'I didn't think they'd foul their own drinking place,' she said. It didn't help when Denis took the cow's part.

'The cow thought it went on the bank, Esmay. It only went into the stream by accident.' As if it mattered why.

'Oh, what will I do?' she wailed. But now, distinctly, she saw smoke from a chimney. 'Look! Over there!

Denis. A cottage. We can ask them for a glass of water.'

'A mug of water, not a glass,' Denis murmured, as he strained to see the hut. 'It may be only a shelter for a herd in lambing time,' he warned.

'They'd have water there all the same,' she insisted, and she began to run in the direction of the smoke. Denis had no option but to follow.

When they came in full view of the hut they would have thought it uninhabited if, apart from the smoke, they had not seen a paint-can with a red geranium in it on the window sill.

'It doesn't look too promising,' Denis said.

'Oh, come on. Let's go to the door,' she cried eagerly.

'Remember, Esmay,' he said, holding her back, 'these people won't understand when you ask for water. They'll want to bring you inside and give you tea – or milk.' At the thought of milk Esmay made a face, and seeing this Denis stressed the point. 'They'll want to bring us in and sit us down to a pot of stewed tea and big doorsteps of brown bread. Maybe an egg! I know what I'm talking about. I've asked for water before now in places like this in Scotland and the Orkneys. And I can tell you that what you'd get there would be a cup of milk warm from the cow!'

'Oh, stop it, Denis!'

'I'm serious. People in backward places like this have strong instincts of hospitality.'

They were almost at the door of the hut when Esmay stopped.

'Do you think the people who live here might be what Professor Merrit called folk people?'

'What are folk people?' Denis asked, surprised. 'I

didn't hear him say anything like that. What did he mean?'

'Oh, I wasn't really listening either,' Esmay said tactfully, 'but I think that's the name given to people who have been living in the one place for generations and who have sustained themselves in the one way for the same length of time.' When Denis looked at her almost in disbelief, Esmay shrugged her shoulders. 'Maybe I read it somewhere,' she said. Then, as they heard a sound within the cottage – a chair being dragged across the dirt floor perhaps – she suddenly hung back. 'Denis? Do you think – ' she began, and then stopped with a shudder. She finished the sentence by an involuntary glance back over her shoulder at the cairn. Reading her mind, Denis shook his head.

'Hardly!' he said. 'There were several waves of migration.'

Suddenly they both became aware of a woman standing in the doorway. They were both startled, since she had appeared quite silently.

The woman was tall and straight-standing, her skin tanned by smoke. She didn't speak, she just stared. Not at Denis, but at Esmay. And when Esmay asked for the water, she turned and still without speaking disappeared again into the smoky interior.

Was she not going to give the water? Esmay's thirst had returned as fierce as fire. It didn't help matters that in a triangle of sunlight cut out on the floor of the cottage, she saw a bucket supported on a chair without a back. It must surely contain fresh water?

Then, to her relief, in the patch of light she saw the woman's feet approach the bucket and heard a vessel dip into water. The sound of that water would have maddened her if the next moment the woman hadn't come out into the open with a brimming mug. But on the threshold, unaccountably, the woman turned again and went back. She must have handed the mug to someone, up to now unseen, and Esmay heard her give an order in a harsh voice. 'Take it out to her.'

Such ungraciousness made Esmay glance nervously at Denis, and in the fraction of time she had taken her eyes off the doorway, a young girl, a girl of her own age and build, glided noiselessly out into the sunlight. In her hand was the mug of water.

Instinctively, as Esmay reached for it, she was vaguely aware of the girl's litheness and grace, of her shiny mane of black hair, and her bare feet. The feet, like the hand that held the mug, were thin-boned and of an eggshell whiteness. The face also, although averted, had a delicate purity of texture.

Esmay actually had the mug in her hand when Denis gasped. And at the sound the young girl turned. Oh, God! The left side of her face was – well, eaten was the word that came to Esmay's mind.

The face was half eaten away. But by what? By fire? Or? Oh, God, could it be by some disease? Lupus? Leprosy? What? As if a spell was put upon her, Esmay could not drag her eyes away from the ravaged flesh. There were no sores, no festering, and over most of the cheek a covering had grown, more membrane than skin, silvery and tautly drawn, and of a sickly silkiness. Whatever had consumed the flesh must have done so a long time ago, and only around the rim of the eye and at the tender edges of the nostril was there any trace of fluid or running. Oh, God. Pity for the girl blinded

Esmay for a moment to her own plight. But only for a moment. Then pity for herself flooded over her. How could she drink from that mug? Reason told her there could be no contagion in those dried scabs, but she knew that if she drank from that mug she'd spend the rest of her life wiping her mouth and spitting out whenever she remembered it.

Desperately she wanted to turn to Denis and ask him what to do, but the woman had come to the door again and her marble eyes were fixed on her, compelling her to drink. By an almost superhuman effort, Esmay wrenched her own eyes free and, turning to the girl, she tried to plead with her for compassion. Had the girl no sympathy for her? Apparently not. In utter despair Esmay raised the mug to her lips.

'Esmay! Don't drink it!' Denis shouted.

'Oh, but – ' How could she refuse? It would cut the girl to the quick.

But, as if the girl and her mother were a million miles away, Denis raised his voice still louder. 'Their feelings don't matter, Esmay. Can't you see that? It's their motive that matters.'

What did he mean? Esmay looked back at the woman, and immediately her eyes were caught again in the toils of that malevolent stare. Then Denis reached out his hand. 'Here, give me a sip, Esmay,' he said, and he took the mug from her. Oh no. No. What she herself was prepared to endure she was not prepared to let him endure for her. If he raised it to his lips she would knock it out of his hand. But, as Denis took the mug, it was the young girl who, like a wildcat, sprang through the air and, clawing at the mug, dashed it to the ground. Staring down at the pieces of broken crockery, Esmay saw that the strong white handle had broken as easily as if it were a whorl of white icing. 'Quick!' Denis grabbed her by the hand, and they began to run down the slope, their feet slithering and at times nearly flying from under them. Their hearts were pounding, and now they had no thought in their heads beyond getting back to the road, to the car, to the farmhouse.

Senility

Ada was steeping her sheets when her daughter surprised her by arriving on her doorstep.

'What on earth are you doing, Mummy?' Laura cried. 'I thought you sent heavy things to the laundry.'

Ada saw no reason to explain that she'd had an accident during the night. 'I didn't hear the car,' she said. 'Did you honk the horn?'

'Of course!'

'Of course,' Ada murmured apologetically. Laura had good reason to be abrupt. She never went by without honking in case Ada needed something from the shops, but Ada, priding herself on never running short mid-week, always ran to the window and signalled that she needed nothing. Laura looked again at the wet sheets. Somehow she guessed what had happened. 'Oh, Mummy, I don't believe it! You must be getting senile,' she said with a laugh. Left to herself Ada would not have seen anything remotely funny about the mishap, but she laughed too. Laura rolled up her sleeves. 'Here, let me wring them out for you,' she said.

'Not at all.' Ada gave her a little push. 'Off you go! I know you have a lot to do.' She went to the door with her. 'I'll be seeing you tonight, I expect?'

'Yes. Me or John,' Laura said. Then from the gate she called back. 'Next week, when you're under the same roof with us, you'll be able to call me during the night whenever anything like this happens.'

'It's hardly going to be a nightly occurrence,' Ada said.

'I didn't mean that,' Laura said and chastened, she got into her car, waved, and drove away.

Ada was a bit rattled by the visit. For one thing, Laura ought to know how she felt about the word senile. It was a word that had for a long time been a source of friction between them, dating from the death of Ada's own mother, who, in her late eighties, had had to be put into a home for the aged because of physical debility. For some reason Laura liked to say the old woman had been mentally disturbed at the end, but apart from their disagreement on this, Laura and Ada got on famously. Ada had no real misgivings about selling her house and going to live with her daughter. Now, rinsing out the sheets, she wrung them again and went out to spread them on the grass.

It was a beautiful day and the garden was at its best. Ada had a momentary pang at the thought of leaving, but the house really was too large for one person living alone. It was only common sense to 'join forces' with the young couple, as John put it so generously, considering she wouldn't be contributing to the household. The young people had no need of money from her. They knew of course that one day all she possessed would belong to them.

A week later, on the day after the sale, John took another morning off to move Ada and her personal belongings. They had arranged to stop off at the bank to lodge the proceeds of the sale, and after they had made the lodgement Ada took the occasion to be explicit about the terms of her will. Then on a sudden impulse she sounded a cautionary note.

'Let's hope there won't be any unexpected demands on my money. I dread the thought that my small resources could be drained away in some tiresome illness.'

'There'll be no fear of that,' John said firmly. 'Laura intends to keep you wrapped up in cotton wool!'

'Thank you, John.' Ada was grateful. 'You realize of course that I like to feel that when I die I'll be leaving you and Laura some token of my love and gratitude.'

'We appreciate that, Ada.' John squeezed her arm. He was more gracious than Laura, who took no interest whatever in this subject. Later that very morning, after John had left Ada off and gone back to the office, Laura was almost rude when Ada attempted to show her pass-book.

'By the time you die, Mummy, your nest-egg will seem very small to John and me – well, relatively small anyway!' And seeing that Ada was hurt by this, she became downright impatient. 'You ought to be glad we don't need any money from you,' she said. The two women were up in the room that was to be Ada's, a very nice room. 'Take my advice, Mummy, and spend your money on yourself.' Leaning over, she gave Ada a very sweet kiss. 'It's time you had it easy,' she said, so lovingly that Ada would have been extraordinarily happy, if the next moment Laura had not spoiled everything. 'Keep well and look after yourself, Mummy. You wouldn't want to be a burden on everyone like poor Grandmother, would you?'

'Your grandmother was never a great burden on me, Laura,' Ada said. 'If I had had more fortitude, I could have kept her at home with us till the end, and not put her into that dreadful place.' She sighed. 'I see that now, when it's too late.'

'Rubbish.' Laura pursed her lips. 'Not after she got –'

'Please! Don't say that word, I beg of you. Not today of all days.'

'What do you mean by that?' Laura stopped gathering up the empty cartons that had contained the few possessions Ada had kept.

'You wouldn't understand,' Ada said. Mercifully, Laura did not press the point any further.

By mid-day the room was as neat and tidy as when it was the spare room, ready at a moment's notice to house an overnight guest.

'I hope you'll be comfortable here, Mummy.' Laura looked around the room. 'If you like, John can move your armchair to face the window. We put it there so you'd have your back to the light for reading, or for taking your nap in the afternoon.'

'But I never take a nap,' Ada protested.

'Oh, I forgot,' Laura said lightly. She went over to the bed and lifted the chintz valance to expose the mattress. 'You ought to sleep well at night, anyway. We got a new mattress.'

Ada felt that this was an unnecessary extravagance, but she didn't say so. Instead she followed Laura downstairs. It was time for lunch.

'Now! How are we going to spend the rest of the day?' Laura asked, when they got up from the table.

'You must attend to your own affairs, dear,' Ada said. 'You've lost a lot of time on me, already.'

'Oh, that's all right, I decided to devote the whole day to you.'

'Ah well, in that case,' Ada said happily, 'why don't we go out in the garden?' She was thinking of the two big boxes of plants and rooted cuttings she'd dug up in her own garden before the sale, and which were in the garage waiting to be planted.

But Laura shivered.

'It's far too cold.'

'Not for me,' Ada said.

'Ah well, I was never as hardy as you, Mummy. But I suppose those plants you brought ought to be put into the ground soon?'

'The sooner the better,' Ada said, 'but, if you like, they could be heeled-in in some sheltered corner, and left till next spring.'

'Oh, could they?' Laura seemed relieved. Then she thought of all the room they were taking up, and she frowned again. 'That would be just as much work as planting them properly.' She glanced out of the window. 'Let's leave them where they are for the moment, anyway.'

The day passed pleasantly for Ada, and that evening, after a very good dinner, she went up to bed deliberately early to give the young people some time to themselves. It was nice to hear the murmur of their voices below as she was dropping off to sleep.

She was, therefore, absolutely mortified to wake in the small hours of that night and find she had had another accident. She sprang out of bed to see what damage she had done. Luckily the mattress had come through safe. She pulled off the bottom sheet and threw it on the floor. Then, stumbling out of her room, she crossed the landing to the linen room, got out a clean sheet and made up the bed again. Once back in bed, she briefly regretted that she hadn't taken Laura up on her offer to bring her breakfast in bed, but she'd felt that the least she could do was to make an appearance before John left the house for the office.

The next morning, Ada ran into Laura on the landing as Laura was hurrying down herself, and although Ada was reluctant to make the disclosure, she did so in a quick whisper.

'The mattress is unharmed though,' she added.

'Oh, bother the mattress!' Laura said. 'It's you I'm concerned about. Why didn't you call me? I could have got you clean sheets.'

'I didn't want to wake you, so I helped myself.'

'Oh?' Laura seemed surprised. 'Where did you find the sheets?'

'In the linen room, of course.'

'I meant on what shelf?' Laura said. 'I try to rotate the linen.'

'I see.' Ada understood, but next minute Laura looked anxiously at her.

'I wonder what's causing this to happen?' she said.

'I'm afraid it's like losing a tooth, or getting one's first grey hair,' Ada said. 'It's an intimation of mortality.'

Laura had to laugh 'Mummy, you're quite a wag. I must tell that to John,' she said.

'Laura! It would be most indelicate to mention this to your husband.'

'Oh dear. I suppose it could be embarrassing for you. I won't say a word.' Together they went down to the breakfast room.

John had finished, and was wiping his mouth with his napkin. He put the napkin down, stood up and pulled out Ada's chair, but when Ada turned to thank him, he was gone.

'He'll be back!' Laura said, and she winked. 'He's as fastidious as a cat about these early-morning matters.'

Ada ate her first really hearty breakfast in years. She felt in fine fettle, and when John came back into the breakfast room, with his coat on, and carrying his hat and briefcase, he gave both women a peck on the cheek. When he was finally gone for good, Laura turned around.

'Well, what are you going to do with yourself today, Mummy?' she asked. 'It's a glorious day! Perhaps we ought to put in those plants you brought?'

'I could put them in alone,' Ada said, but Laura wouldn't hear of it.

'I don't get nearly enough fresh air,' she said.

She did look pale, Ada thought, but again she forbore from saying what she thought. She hoped her own zeal for gardening might become contagious. And indeed, all that week, Laura did spend a lot of time out of doors with her. The days flew. Even when Laura wasn't with her, the time went fast because there was so much to do. The garden was not neglected, but Laura and John had no feeling for plants and no interest whatever in texture or tone, or the need for contrasting effects. Ada worked like a trooper, but she took care not to make any large-scale alterations, although when, on occasion, she did nervously make a change, Laura and John neither noticed nor cared. Day by day, Ada became happier.

Then, about six months after she'd moved in with them, Ada had another mishap. This time she was devastated. Again she sprang out of bed in an agony of concern for the bedding, but there was no real harm done. Once again she pulled off the wet sheet, and once again she staggered out to the linen closet, wishing she'd asked Laura to explain her system of rotation. But the door of the linen room was locked! Ada had no recourse but to go back to her room and make the best of things, wrapping herself up in a cocoon of blankets. When she woke again it was morning, and the house was stirring into life. Scrambling into her clothes, she threw the coverlet over the bed and left the room. On the stairs, she met her daughter, who was running back up to get a clean handkerchief for her husband. Ada didn't stop to tell her about the incident. Yet she had barely taken her place at the table, and said good morning to John, when Laura stormed back into the breakfast room.

'Not again, Mummy! What on earth is the matter?'

Ada gave Laura a stony look and turned to her son-in-law, but he was slipping away from the table. Her only option was to face her daughter.

'What brought you into my room anyway?' she asked. 'I thought you were running up to get a clean handkerchief for your husband?' Laura pointed to where, beside her plate, a neatly folded handkerchief waited, presumably to be given in exchange for a soiled, and no doubt disgusting, one which John would produce and hand over to her on returning to the room.

Not across the table, Ada prayed. Not across the food! Then her mind returned to her problem. 'There's no need for you to interfere,' she said. 'I can attend to the matter myself. I would have done so already, only the door of the linen room was locked. Against whom, may I ask?'

'Oh, don't be so touchy,' Laura said.

Ada heard her son-in-law's footsteps approaching. 'Let's drop the subject,' she said.

John came into the room all smiles.

'Good-bye, girls. Have a good day.'

After they heard his car drive away, the two women were somewhat constrained.

'Is there more coffee in that thing?' Ada asked at last, deliberately disparaging the pretty little porcelain coffee-pot, the daily use of which she secretly respected.

Laura poured her another cup. 'Is that hot? I could make more.'

'No. This is all right.' Ada was not to be blandished. 'You didn't tell me why you went into my room? I know this is your house, but surely I'm allowed the privacy of my bedroom?'

'Oh, Mummy. Don't be mean! I was worried about you.'

'Nonsense,' Ada said.

'But this is happening so *often*.'

'I'd like to know what you consider often?' Ada said hotly, and this, she was glad to see, broke down Laura's reserves.

'Oh, Mummy, darling,' the girl cried. 'I couldn't bear it if anything happened to you. It would break my heart.'

Ada looked away.

'Anyone would think the world was coming to an end,' she said. She stood up. 'What about that sheet? Give it to me.'

'I'll get it,' Laura said humbly. 'And I'll help you make the bed.' She glanced out of the window. It was another glorious day. 'Let's go out in the garden. Do you remember when we were putting in those pinks, you said that after they took root we could take slips from them – slips or cuttings or whatever it is they're called.'

It pleased Ada beyond measure to have Laura defer to her gardening skill, but she did not jump at the suggestion. 'Let's attend to the bed first,' she said in a practical fashion.

When the bed was made and they had tidied up the room, Laura took the crumpled sheet and dumped it in the laundry bin.

'Shouldn't we rinse it?' Ada asked.

Laura shrugged her shoulders.

'Why bother! Let's wash the breakfast dishes and then go out in the sun and enjoy ourselves.'

It was Laura, though, who was unable to forget.

'Are you sure you're all right, Mummy?' she asked, not once but twice, while they were washing up the breakfast things. In the end Ada found her own mind straying back to the indignity of the night.

'Oh, Laura,' she cried out of her thoughts. 'How I hate to think of the humiliation your grandmother must have suffered at the hands of those nurses. They were wholly lacking in delicacy.'

'It's too late to worry about it now,' Laura said easily. 'Grandmother was too far gone for niceties, anyway.'

'On the contrary!' Ada said sharply. 'She was too quick by half! Do you know, it's my belief, Laura, that deep down she regarded that place as a kind of workhouse, and I think she cherished a secret grudge against me for putting her there.'

'If that's the case, then she was a fool,' Laura said bluntly. 'And you're a worse fool to let it bother you, particularly when she was – '

'Laura! *Please!* Your grandmother was sharp and bright in her mind up to the very end. Let me tell you something that happened in that place not long before she died.' The incident Ada had in mind suddenly brought tears to her eyes. 'The poor little thing,' she said.

'For heaven's sake, Mummy! I thought you'd come to terms with yourself about all that business.'

'No, dear. No.' Ada said. 'I mean, yes. Yes,' she said hastily, correcting herself. 'I have come to terms with myself, but what I'm going to tell you underlines the limitations of those geriatric units. You see, when I went to visit your grandmother, I used to creep into the ward on tiptoe in case the other old women were dozing, as they usually were, but one day when I'd crept in, what do you think I found? Bedlam! Standing beside your grandmother's bed, one on either side, were two young nurses laughing their heads off. Not nice laughing either. Ugly, vulgar laughing.'

'What were they laughing at?'

'That's what I wanted to know,' Ada said. 'They were behaving like ward-maids. They'd just taken up your grandmother's newspaper – you remember of course that I used to have the daily paper sent in to her? She always liked to glance at it, although towards the end I used to find it wrapped at the foot of her bed, because nobody had bothered to unwrap it. If anyone had gone to the trouble of unrolling it and flattening it out, I'm sure she would have shown some interest in it.' Here, however, Ada stopped short. 'Laura! I hope you read the daily paper, or at least run your eye over the editorials, because –' Ada stopped again. 'What was I saying, dear?'

'Something about two ward-maids?'

'No, Laura, no. They weren't ward-maids, they were trained nurses. Trained indeed! I'm afraid their training left a lot to be desired. Nowhere on earth is as noisy as a hospital, and it is the nurses that make all the noise, banging things about and talking at the top of their voices. As for those trolleys they wheel around at meal-times, laden with metal trays! Why metal? Tell me that! Your grandmother used to wince with pain – actual pain – at that sound. But that was nothing to what some of the other patients had to suffer. I remember particularly those poor bloated women in the other beds – obese, that's the medical word for them, although gross would be my word. But, anyway, God help them, did you know that when the nurses were making their beds, or had to turn them over to change a dressing, they used to call in the porter to lift them? Think of that for humiliation. Your grandmother was not heavy. On the contrary, she was too slight, too fragile – which, by the way, was probably why she never, as far as I know, suffered from bed sores – but her bones were brittle, breakable as glass I was told. When they went to give her a bath, they still had to get the porter to lift her in and out of the tub. When she told me this I tried to pretend to her they were male nurses, but I know she didn't believe me. Laura! Are you listening?'

'Yes, of course,' Laura said, 'but get on with it, Mummy! What were the silly bitches doing?'

'Bitches. Oh, you mean the nurses. It was what they were saying I minded – that, and their ugly sniggering. They had your grandmother pitifully perplexed. And as you know Laura, where the aged are concerned, perplexity can be a severe mental anguish which –'

'Never mind the theorizing, Mummy. Get on with the story.'

Ada hastened to comply. 'Those dreadful women had for once opened your grandmother's newspaper, but they were holding it up in front of her and quizzing her about a picture on the front page. "*Who is that? I suppose you know him too? I suppose he is another of your daughter's friends, or your grand-daughter's?*" The ignorant creatures couldn't conceive that any patient in that ward could possibly be acquainted with a person of prominence in the outside world. And there was your poor little grandmother, who didn't even have her glasses on, peering at the paper and nodding her head because, as a matter of fact, although she could not recall the name, she did recognize the picture. She did know the person in question.'

'Oh, really? Who was it?' For the first time Laura looked genuinely interested.

'Oh, the name doesn't matter,' Ada said impatiently. 'It's slipped my own mind for the moment. But you should have seen with what civility she was treating those ill-bred creatures, with what dignity she was comporting herself –' Here Ada was overcome by an access of anguish. 'Oh, Laura, how could I have put her in that place? How could I have abandoned her, left her at the mercy of such people? The other patients could give her no consolation. They were moribund old women for the most part, comatose. They were no fit company for her. How she must have missed all the fascinating people you brought to the house when you were still living at home. She loved company. And what good company she was herself when she was on form. But those nurses – oh, they were foxy. When they saw me, those were the very words they used to try to cover up their callousness. "She's such good company," they said. "Such good fun." Fun?'

Laura said nothing for a moment. Then she put her hand on Ada's and stroked it gently. 'Don't you think, Mummy, that a bit of fun might have been a welcome change in that ward – for all concerned?'

It was so sweet to have her daughter stroke her hand, Ada was prepared to compromise.

'I suppose I didn't think of it in that light. And of course your grandmother herself always appreciated light-hearted people.' But the next minute remorse returned and engulfed her. 'She must have been starved for companionship,' she said. Immediately Laura stopped stroking her hand.

'Oh, for God's sake, Mummy! Stop torturing your-self – '

'Torturing myself?'

' – and me!' Laura said. 'Oh, why can't you face it, grandmother *was* senile.'

The word was out at last, but Ada clapped her hands over her ears as if she was still in time to protect herself from hearing it.

'Thank God your poor grandmother can't hear you.'

'Don't be absurd! I would never have said such a thing in her hearing although, mind you, I think she might have cackled at the good of it. It's amazing how nature has cures for its own ills, and in her case the decay – '

'Decay?' Ada would have liked to block her ears again, but instead she retreated into herself. Wait till your own turn comes, miss! she thought. Then she had a wild impulse to yell this out, but she resisted. Instead tears flashed into her eyes, and although Laura despised tears, Ada could do nothing to stop them from falling. They splashed down on her hands.

'I'm sorry dear,' she murmured.

'Please, Mummy!' Laura was, as Ada expected, furious. Just then, however, from Laura herself uncontrollably too, a sigh broke, sudden and loud like a hiccup, taking both of them by surprise.

Ada immediately took out her handkerchief and mopped her face. Laura walked over to the window.

Ada followed her daughter with her eyes. The garden was blazing with a sunlight that had gained in strength and brilliance since she'd looked out last. Ada had an urge to rush out at once in case that sun was too bright to last. But here Laura made a false move, heaving a second sigh which, unlike the first one, was not at all involuntary but of the deep and deliberate variety, intended perhaps to do for the heart what on occasion retching can do for the stomach – relieve it of too heavy a load.

'Mummy! For goodness' sake, come out to the garden,' she said, 'and show me how to take those cuttings. I'd love to be able to do it without depending on you.'

Ada thought that was a bit tactless for a daughter to say to a mother, but then Laura said something very nice.

'Would you believe it, Mummy, I never knew until the day of the sale, when I heard you telling the people who bought the house, that you yourself had propagated all those masses of pinks we had edging the paths in our garden at home. I always thought you'd bought them – paid a fortune for them!' Ada could not keep a smile from forming around her eyes and Laura quickly took advantage of it. 'Those masses of pinks were the bestest thing I've ever seen in any garden,' she said.

'Thank you, darling.' The babyish superlative her daughter had used was forever associated in her mind with the days when Laura was a tot, running around the old garden, gentle and biddable and seeming at times to float like thistledown among the flowers. Nevertheless, when her daughter proffered a hand to assist her to her feet, she brushed it away.

'I want you to know that I realize, of course, that in advanced age there is sometimes a diminution of powers, due to hardening of the arteries. But this doesn't necessarily impair the faculties, it just causes a momentary stoppage in the memory – a stoppage frequently unnoticed by the person herself, and often not noticeable to her listeners, either. The truth is that this can happen to anyone. And at any age!' There! Having got that off her chest Ada would have let the matter rest there, but Laura turned away as if the conversation was at an end, and started to look for something in a drawer of the sideboard, giving a distinct impression of dismissing everything that had been said between them that morning. Ada frowned. Surely that wasn't where they kept the garden clippers? And surely Laura knew you used your fingers to take a cutting? Ada's temper flared up again like a blaze through twigs. 'It may interest you to know, Laura,' she said, 'that hardening of the arteries has been known to set in as early as the mid thirties, or even the early thirties.'

Triumphant at last, Ada swept across the room to the glass door that led into the garden.

In the garden, however, she wasn't happy – not at all happy. For the remainder of the morning – and there wasn't much left of it – she was the one who was silent, while Laura chattered away uncharacteristically and almost inconsequentially, trying no doubt to make amends for her disagreeableness earlier. As usual, she overdid things. 'Are you sure it's all right for you to be working so hard?' she asked. As if work in a garden was ever easy! 'Why don't you take this fork, it's lighter.' As if a light fork was of any use! And when they went inside for lunch and Laura asked if she'd like a cushion behind her back, Ada lost her temper.

'Ah, leave me alone,' she said, whereupon, of course, Laura got huffy.

'I don't see why you object that your daughter – your only child – should venture to suggest you might be well advised to realize your age and take better care of yourself!'

'That depends on what you mean by care?' Ada said cautiously.

'Well, for one thing, you might consider having a check-up,' Laura said, her candid eyes betraying no awareness of the impertinence of this suggestion.

'In my opinion,' Ada said irritably, 'having a medical check-up is only looking for trouble.'

'Sometimes a slight adjustment can help to avoid trouble later on – major trouble,' Laura said ominously.

'But surely that is my business?' Ada said.

'Is it?'

'Yes, it is,' Ada said, quite simply, and to her astonishment Laura was quelled. They proceeded amicably enough with the lunch after that, although when they went out again Laura was a lot less talkative. Ada didn't mind because, as the late afternoon sun gilded the flowers and gave them a deeper glow, her thoughts returned to her own garden and dwelt there. By evening, she had paid the price of this indulgence. She was saturated with sadness. So, at dusk, when John got home, she was glad to go indoors with the young people. As she hurried upstairs to change for supper, she could hear the others talking in their own room, and listening to the sound of their voices she was taken out of herself and restored to a happier frame of mind.

While she was running a comb through her hair, as a last minute touch preparatory to going down, Laura came into her room without knocking.

'Look here, Mummy!' She said, without preamble, 'perhaps if you won't listen to me, you will listen to John! He agrees with me. He thinks there may well be nothing wrong with you, but he says you owe it to me to see a doctor, just to put my mind at rest about you. He says you have a duty to me in this respect.'

Ada turned away in annoyance. So Laura had betrayed her? Such disloyalty from one's own flesh and blood was staggering. Daughter or no daughter, at that moment what Ada felt towards Laura was pure hatred. She would dearly have liked to give her a slap. Since one could not very well give a grown woman a slap, she was suddenly inspired to take a swipe at John.

'If your husband is so fond of doctors,' she said, enunciating each syllable with deadly precision, 'then why doesn't he get his antrums cleaned out? That, if you like, is a slight operation, hardly to be called an operation at all, except that it is a fairly painful business, I believe, because it has to be done without an anaesthetic. I'd say it would be worth it, though, if it put a stop to that ugly sniffling and snuffling of his – especially at night. Not that I mind, although if I did, I'd be in no position to complain, would I?' Here, however, Ada's venom shamed even herself and inwardly she collapsed. Outwardly she kept up a good front. 'Don't expect me to go down to dinner after this,' she said, 'I'm not much good at pretence!'

No sooner had she said this, however, than Ada realized how little she'd eaten at lunch due to being upset then too. She had been literally starving since mid-afternoon. She hadn't really expected Laura to take her at her word. When the girl stalked out Ada's only consolation was to rush over to the door, and bang it shut. Then she sat down on the side of the bed and began to go back over what she was still determined to regard as accidents. Why did they happen?

Painstakingly, she tried to find a cause for each case. Since the first time, she had been taking the obvious precaution of cutting down her intake of fluids, especially towards evening. Ruefully, she remembered how, when she was first married, Patrick used to be amazed at the quantities of water she drank in the course of a day. As well as that, she used to bring a carafe of water up to their bedroom at night, a carafe which she would empty to the last drop before morning without any ill consequences. She was young then, of course, but surely if her kidneys had developed a weakness since then, it would have made itself manifest by day as well as by night? But no, she never suffered any inconvenience whatever during the daytime, neither on long journeys nor at the theatre, whereas some of her contemporaries could on occasion be a real nuisance. What then was the matter? She ate well. She slept well. Furthermore, sleep usually brought with it a proliferation of dreams – a sign of a sound mind in a sound body, or so she understood, having been told that it was firmly established by modern medics that in their dreams people got rid of their hang-ups. Her own dreams were always diverting – vivid and crammed with incident. And since she had come to live with Laura she had been keeping a pencil and pad on her bedside table to jot down as much as she could remember of a dream immediately on waking, because John enjoyed hearing her relate them. Ah, well! She'd better try to put her problem out of her mind for this night, and get into bed before she became so ravenous she would go down and make up with Laura.

When Ada settled herself between the sheets and

switched off the bedside light, she was, at once, in the domain of dreams or, it would be more correct to say, she was at the gateway to that domain, because there was always a moment when, if a dream threatened to be disagreeable or scary, she could, at will, hold back and refuse to enter. But tonight the prospect that opened before her was full of wonder. She abandoned herself to it with joy.

To begin with, she was young again. And more joyous still, she was again with Laura's father.

'Oh, Patrick, did you hear what I called you?' she cried, because Laura could not possibly have been born then. They were on their honeymoon in the beautiful Villa Plaisance that a friend had lent them. Patrick laughed.

'Our baby may not be born yet, but she may be conceived,' he said, and they laughed for joy at the thought. And it might well have been true: they were two months married at the time, and nearing the end of their honeymoon. She knew this because, in the dream, Patrick had a time-table and was working out a schedule for their return journey. It might even have been their last day in Plaisance for, evidently not wanting to waste a second of the precious sun that poured down on the villa and surrounding country, they had decided to go outdoors and work on their schedule in a little wood behind the villa.

They had never been in this wood before – well, it wasn't exactly a wood, just a clump of trees that had no doubt been planted as a windbreak to keep the salt sea breezes from scorching the lawns. To their surprise, under the trees everywhere, the ground was carpeted with flowers like the forests in medieval tapestries. Not with primroses and bluebells, though, such as one might expect to find in a wood at home, but with cyclamens – myriads of rosy cyclamens. Neither she nor Patrick had ever seen such a breathtaking sight. At home wild flowers were soft, floppy, quick to wilt and spill their seeds, but these cyclamens looked hard as marble. Adamantine was the word that sprang to Ada's mind. She saw that on some of the corms the seeds that had already formed were raised up on wiry stems, tightly coiled and bent inward, as if to ensure an economy rather than a diffusion of seed. This colony of flowers was evidently of great antiquity. Some of the corms were so old and crusty they jutted over the ground like outcroppings of volcanic basalt. You couldn't walk through them without risk of twisting your ankle. At last, Patrick found a patch of thin grass and sat down; he produced the time-table, patting the ground beside him.

'Sit down, Ada. There's plenty of room. Sit down,' he said.

Ada was just about to sit down when at that moment she experienced a most irritating need of nature, *un petit besoin* as the French neatly put it.

'Just a second, Patrick! Sorry for being a nuisance, I'll have to run back to the house,' she said.

'Whatever for?' Patrick stared at her. She wasn't shy with him about something so natural, but she had noticed that he himself was reticent, or should she say respectful, of these small privacies, so she didn't answer. But he guessed.

'Why trudge back?' He pointed to the trees and laughed. 'What are trees for?'

'Oh Patrick!' She laughed too, but she was uneasy because, in the queer way that things switch in dreams, the trees had become sparse and spindly, and offered no concealment. The villa, on the other hand, had come close and it seemed to be all windows. If anyone looked out she would be seen distinctly. But by now the need to relieve herself was so pressing she had no choice but to run.

'Over there! Quick! Behind those laurels,' Patrick said, and she made for the cover, stumbling over the corms and treading the flowers into the ground. But now, everything had altered and the cyclamens were no longer real flowers, but glittering trinkets sharply edged and strong. They came to no harm under her feet.

Barely in time she reached the laurels, and pulled up her skirt. Oh, what bliss it was when the warmth of the sun was merged with a new warmth that rose up in vapour from the ground and seemed to bathe her whole body with moisture.

Oh God! Ada woke with a start. She sprang out of bed, but it was too late, and she sank down on the side of the bed. It was broad daylight and downstairs she heard the clatter of cups. The others were already at breakfast. Frantically, she wondered if she dared steal out on to the landing to see if the door of the linen closet might by chance have been left unlocked; she could snatch a pair of clean sheets, and bundle the others somewhere out of sight until she could get them to a laundry. But immediately she abandoned this hopeless project. Instead she went down on her knees and covered her face with her hands.

'Lord, Lord,' she prayed. 'Don't make it too hard

on me.' Then suddenly, uncovering her face, she got to her feet and went over to the window. Drawing back the curtains, she stood looking down into the garden. Then, without kneeling, she amended her prayer. 'Don't make it too hard on Laura, I mean.'

Eterna

Out in the street at last, the doctor stopped running and looked back at the steps of the gallery. The woman was not following him. All the same, he went across to where the car was parked. But as there was still no sign of her he didn't drive away. His wife would be along shortly – she was only picking up odds and ends for the kids at some shop around the corner where there was a closing-down sale. What a fool he was to have gone into that cursed gallery. Just because he had found a parking place opposite it! If he'd bought an evening paper and waited for Annie in the car, he'd have saved himself a nasty fright, because now he felt certain that the crazy woman could not possibly have been Eterna. Not in those outlandish clothes! Not with that daft look in her eyes as she strayed from painting to painting, causing everyone to stare.

If it was Eterna, wouldn't he have noticed her the minute he went into the place, instead of merely turning to see why other people were staring? Even then, he wouldn't have given the poor soul a second glance if he hadn't fancied a resemblance. But when he found her eyes fixed on him he lost his head and ran, although he was vaguely aware, even then, that her daft gaze had already wandered away from him. That was another thing. If it was Eterna, wouldn't she have recognized him?

It was mortifying to think that he had lost control to such an extent that he *ran*. Supposing one of his patients had been there and seen him. It was unlikely, though, that anyone up from the country for a precious half day in Dublin would waste time in the National Gallery. He relaxed. He lit a cigarette and settled down to wait for Annie.

Why had he gone into the gallery at all? He had probably fallen into a nostalgic mood, thinking of all the exhibitions he'd attended there before he was qualified and when he still entertained notions of a practice in Dublin. In those days, going to art exhibitions, symphony concerts, operas, and that sort of thing seemed as important for his advancement as going to his lectures. Ah, well, he'd better not tell Annie about his little adventure. Not that she'd give a damn whether it was Eterna or not – she'd be concerned only at his having gone into the gallery at all, at his backsliding into intellectual snobbery, or what she called professional posturing. 'Tommyrot' was the word she had actually used the first time he met her, or, rather the first time they had had what could be considered a real conversation.

'It's not as if you were a specialist,' she had said bluntly. 'A district doctor doesn't have to put on airs like the bigwigs up in Dublin. That kind of thing might impress Dublin people, but it won't go down in a country town, it will only do you harm. The people in this town are simple, but they are not fools. They see through you, Doctor, the way they see through a pane of glass.' She had looked at him so contemptuously that he winced. But she kept on. 'You know damn well, Doctor, that you wouldn't have deigned to talk to me tonight if you weren't in such a state over that silly nun.'

That had cut through to the bone. It was so true. He had never taken the slightest notice of her before that night, had hardly looked in her direction. In the four months he'd been in the Central Hotel, where she was receptionist, he had hardly spoken a word to her beyond the meagre civilities of good night and good morning. Anyway, she was seldom to be seen except behind the brass grille of her dark little office at the back of the entrance hall. To him, she was just another dreary feature of the broken-down, third-rate hotel.

He himself only spent weekdays in the place. Saturday always saw him hitting out for Dublin. He never bothered to hunt for decent accommodation in the town, being certain that such was not to be found. The whole town was a cultural desert – although, mind you, he knew he was lucky to get his appointment, considering his marks in the Finals. All the same, if he had been lucky he might have got a town with more to offer than the Central Hotel.

It was a dump. The lounge was small and dark, with frosted glass in the windows, and the fire in the shallow grate was kept so tightly banked down with clinkers that once when he threw an orange peel on top of the coals it was still unconsumed when he came back from his rounds at the end of the day. As for the company! It seldom varied – a few commercial travellers, a bank clerk or two, and an elderly, unmarried schoolteacher. If an occasional tourist appeared, he or she very shortly became aware of being misplaced, and accordingly sat all evening in disgruntled silence. He himself had no alternative but to engage in the inanities that passed for conversation and then retire to his dismal bedroom and lie on his bed.

When the call first came to go up to the convent, he was at his lowest. It was a cold night in February, a dreadful night of wind and rain, yet he was glad to get away from the hotel for an hour or so. Admittedly, too, the week that followed gave a bit of spice to his life, but the good was taken out of that by the hideous embarrassment he brought upon himself on his last visit up there.

Back at the Central after that last visit, scarcely tasting the miserable evening meal, he had left the dining room with a vague intention of stepping out in the fresh air. He saw it was raining. And it was as he turned back that he saw the receptionist – Annie – coming out of her box at the back of the hall and taking her coat from the rack.

'It's raining. Did you know that?' he asked. She answered by merely indicating that the coat was a mackintosh, and this made him feel so foolish that he had to detain her to correct the bad impression he'd made. From the few curt words he drew out of her, he gathered that she went for a walk at that hour every evening regularly, wet or fine.

'There's not much else to do, I grant you that,' he said bitterly.

'Oh, I enjoy my walks,' she protested, and then, to his astonishment, she came out with a vehement attack on him. 'Of course, I don't claim to have your sophisticated tastes!' she said, and when he asked what she meant by that remark she shrugged her shoulders. That really provoked him. He hurried after her to the door.

'Do you ever take anyone with you?' he asked. And when, again, she gave no answer he took it she had no objection. Grabbing his own coat from the rack, he stepped out after her into the dark street. The rain had eased off. She had a strong stride and she held up her face as if she liked the slap of the wet, cold air.

The town was badly lit, but when they got out of it, and the stars began to pierce the sky, he found that he enjoyed striding along beside her. They didn't talk much and soon he forgot about the nuns – until they came to a point where the road forked, and Annie, who was slightly ahead, took the one that went past the convent. He stopped.

'Let's not go that way,' he said abruptly.

'Why not? It's the way I always go.' She stopped, too, and he thought she was deferring to him, but he was wrong.

'What's the matter with going this way?' she demanded. Then and there, he blurted out what had happened at the convent that afternoon.

He could not have told a better person. To begin with, Annie had at once dismissed Eterna as silly, and not worth consideration. Then she turned on him. 'If you ask me, you got what you deserved – a good come-down,' she said. And she proceeded from that to give him the worst bawling out he'd had in his life. 'You may be a good doctor, but you won't cut much ice in this town unless you change your tune,' she said, and although the mixed metaphor made him wince, she was obviously so sincere that he listened to her with respect. When she put it to him flatly that he would not have stopped to speak to her if he hadn't been upset, he made no attempt at denial.

'I did not deserve that you should be so kind to me,' he said quietly. He was glad to see, however, that this disconcerted her.

'Well . . . if you're enjoying the walk . . .' she murmured, and moved on again. But he noticed that when they were passing the convent gates she began to talk more animatedly, and he felt she was hoping to distract him. She didn't altogether succeed, but he was grateful to her, and by the time they got back to the Central he certainly felt better than when he had set out. He asked if he might perhaps accompany her the following night. She gave her consent, and after that they went walking every evening.

It wasn't long until he gave up going to Dublin at the week-ends. And before the end of the year they were married. Naturally, after their first conversation, he felt no further need to mention Eterna, and Annie didn't bring her name up, either, except once, when they were on their honeymoon. She told him she had heard that Eterna had left the convent.

'But don't let it bother you!' she added, seeing that he was a bit upset at the news. 'You flatter yourself if you think her decision had anything to do with you. You'll never see her again. She's left the town.'

He put the whole incident out of his mind. Indeed, he tried to forget everything about those awful months before he met Annie. It was the most miserable time in his entire existence. The incident with Eterna was a fitting climax to it.

The night he first saw her, the night he was called to
the convent, was wet and miserable. It was freezing
cold, and the rain was as fierce as hail. It lashed at the
windows of the car, and his flesh anticipated the cas-
cade of icy raindrops that would be dashed over his
hands when he dragged at the massive gates to gain
admission to the long, dark avenue.

He'd been up there twice before – once to inoculate
a group of nuns leaving for the missions, and once to
sign the death certificate of an old lay sister. On both
of those occasions, though, it had been daytime. Now,
in the darkness, the twisting drive seemed endless.
Several times he swerved when he ought to have gone
straight. From time to time wet laurels slapped against
the sides of his car, and a hazy light over the far-off
convent door seemed to shift position, because when
the wind swayed the branches it seemed it was not
them but the light that moved. The gleam of that light
was eerie, and he was reminded of how he used to quake
as a child, listening to tales of a light that flickered over
the bogs and lured the unwary to extinction in bottom-
less holes full of black water. By the time he reached
the convent door, he was completely unnerved. To
make matters worse, before he had a chance to ring
the bell the door was opened by a small bundle in black
who was obviously on the wait for him. It was a lay
sister so doubled up by age and rheumatism that she
was almost on all fours. She had to crane her neck up-
wards to bid him enter. What a cross old face! Yet at
the time he took no exception to her. As far as he was
concerned, that was the look of true sanctity. He'd
seen it often on the faces of lay sisters in hospital wards
and in homes for old people, where it was the lay

sisters, and not the haughty choir nuns, who did all the hard work. He'd often said that if he were God he would not trade a single one of those cranky creatures for a whole conventful of the other sort.

'It's a bad night, Sister,' he said, more amicably than he felt, as he went to help her close the heavy door. But without his help she slammed it shut, and he began to feel that his amiability was superfluous. Ostentatiously, the old woman wiped her bone-dry slippers on a fibre mat inside the door, and bobbing her head for him to follow, she set off with a remarkable gait, for one so old and deformed, across floorboards that were dangerously overwaxed.

Assuming that his patient would be confined to her cell, he looked uneasily at the steep staircase that rose up as bare and ominous as a glass hill, when, to his relief, the old nun came to a stop before reaching it and threw open the door of a parlour to the left. Even then, he thought he was being shown in there to wait for his patient to be brought to him. But she was already there. Sitting stiffly on a straight-backed chair, with her hands primly folded on her lap and her eyes downcast, was how he first saw Eterna.

Eterna? Why was it that from the start his mind discarded the prefix that connoted her dedicated state? She was still only a novice. She was wearing a white veil, but that, of course, did not exonerate him. The truth was that the moment he first laid eyes on her he experienced a most unprofessional desire to humiliate her. Perhaps it was because in spite of her outward appearance of meekness she had instantly conveyed – to him, at least – an impression of unspeakable arrogance. 'All I ask is martyrdom,' she seemed to say, and left it to the old lay sister to explain why a doctor had been called. She had apparently cut her arm.

'Roll up your sleeve and show the cut to the doctor. Hurry up, Sister,' said the old nun, and when Eterna's white fingers fumbled ineffectually with the masculine-looking studs on her wristband the old nun reached out impatiently and rolled up the sleeve with her own crabbed, red hands. When, however, the tender white skin of her arm was bared, Eterna blushed. Good, he thought, as he bent to examine the cut. This might teach her that high aspirations do not turn human beings into angels overnight.

The cut was not deep, but the skin around it was inflamed and angry-looking. There being no antibiotics in those days, he honestly thought at first that it might be necessary to get his patient into a hospital, but, suspecting that this would cause consternation in the community, he decided to dress the cut and see how it would be after a couple of hours.

'Can we get some hot water, Sister, please?' he asked, and when the old nun went over and tugged at a leather bellpull beside the door he understood that the water would be brought. While waiting for it, he told the pair that he would like to call back in three hours. 'At eleven,' he added, to clarify matters. The nuns looked at each other in some confusion.

'The rule of silence is enjoined on us at nine o'clock, Doctor,' the old nun said with severity.

If he had been strictly honest, he would have admitted to himself that, providing the arm was kept motionless, another examination could wait until morning. But a curious obstinacy had taken possession of him. With a stony look, he conceded an hour. 'Ten at the earliest,' he said.

The two veils, the white and the black, veered together like sails in a storm, and the nuns whispered urgently. From a word caught here and there, he gathered that the Reverend Mother had retired to her cell. To whom would they look for guidance and direction? To comply with his wishes, it might be necessary to get the assent of the chaplain, who occupied a cottage in the grounds. But would the Reverend Father be available at that hour? A second session of whispering took place. Perhaps the matter was not grave enough to justify disturbing the priest? More whispering. Finally, the old nun, whose name was Sister Bernadine, fixed him with steely eyes and said that in the extreme emergency she was herself prepared to give the permission necessary for the late call although she was clearly in a state of perturbation.

Putting away his thermometer and closing his bag, the doctor looked disapprovingly at the novice. 'How did you get this cut anyway?' he asked curtly. It was a measure of the effect she'd had on him that he had omitted to ask this routine question at the proper time. And since neither nun had volunteered the information, he began to suspect that the accident was not sympathetically viewed by the rest of the community.

'Tell the doctor what happened, Sister,' said old Bernadine. He thought he detected a note of malice in her voice.

'I fell off a step-ladder, Doctor,' Eterna said, her voice painfully low.

He raised his eyebrows. 'Oh? Are you a carpenter?' he asked, with mock surprise, it being his experience that nuns were forever scrambling up step-ladders and climbing on to tables and chairs to disfigure their convents with shrines and grottoes. 'How did it get infected? And why didn't you bandage it – or don't you believe in remedying bodily ailments?'

'I think perhaps I may have let some turpentine soak through the bandage,' Eterna whispered, her voice now almost impossible to hear.

'Turpentine? Step-ladders? So you really are a sort of handyman hereabouts?' he said, with a cynical smile he could not control.

He turned back to the old nun. 'What exactly happened?' he asked.

She gave him a surly look. 'Sister is an artist, Doctor. She was painting a replica of Our Lady of Good Counsel on the wall of the chapel.' Clearly, such goings on were not her notion of proper behaviour for nuns. 'Our present Superior believes talent may be put to use – but only in the service of God, of course!'

He was taken aback. An artist? He stared at Eterna. To think that this was the first person of talent he had encountered since he came to the district – and she had to be a nun! He felt cheated.

'I should have been told of this earlier,' he said disagreeably. 'I would have kept a closer watch on my words. Artists are such sensitive souls.'

Then, as if Eterna were incapable of understanding, much less executing, his orders, he wrote out a prescription and handed it to the old sister. 'Have that filled in the morning, and meanwhile see that the cut is kept open. Put hot poultices on it, and change them frequently. I'll be back in two hours.' He went towards the door. There, however, he turned and, staring at the novice, added a rider to his orders. 'Water as hot as the patient can stand,' he said. 'How about martyrdom now,' his eyes seemed to ask her as he allowed himself to be let out into the dark by Sister Bernadine.

He had by then only one thought in his head, and that was to be finished with the case. The next two hours dragged, and he thought the time would never come to be back and be done with the tiresome business. Nevertheless, when he did get back, and asked Bernadine for more hot water, it crossed his mind that at that hour everyone else might be asleep, and she might have to amble off and fetch it herself. He felt a strange elation at the thought of being alone with Eterna. But little he knew of convent life! Never in a million years would he be left alone with a novice. The old nun reached for the bellpull, as before, and the hot water was brought immediately. He gave his attention to the cut.

He was glad he had insisted on seeing it again. The swelling had not gone down. He pressed out some pus, put on a dressing, reminded them to get the prescription filled first thing next morning, and said he would call again the following afternoon.

That afternoon of his third call, old Bernadine, as before, was close on the heels of her charge, and kept so close to her throughout the visit that she considerably hampered his movements. He repeatedly had to ask her to get out of his way. 'Excuse me, Sister. . . . If you please, Sister. . . . Pardon me, please.' To his further annoyance, when he did manage to attend to the cut, and was about to leave, the old nun stopped him.

'Will this be your last visit, Doctor?' she asked.

The danger of septicaemia was by then almost negligible, but he decided to be on the safe side. 'I'm afraid not, Sister. One can never be too careful in some matters.' He said it ironically, because the old woman had conveyed the impression that they were all three engaged in an operation highly dangerous to faith and morals! 'I'll be back in two days,' he said.

He intended that fourth visit to be his last. He could have devised no further pretext for calling – the healing process had definitely started. When he arrived at the convent, however, a small change occurred in the order of events, and the door was opened not by Bernadine but by a nun so old that, by comparison, Bernadine could be considered sprightly. This old crone was so doddering that she misapprehended the nature of his visit, and taking him to be the chaplain bearing the Host, blessed herself at sight of him and genuflected.

'This way, Father,' she said reverentially, and he had to manoeuvre her towards the parlour, where Eterna sat sedately. The saintly old soul settled herself down in an armchair that almost swallowed her alive, and took up her beads. In a second, she was lost to this world. Passing the big wooden beads between forefinger and thumb as if she were fashioning pellets of bread, or rolling pills, her whispered Paters and Aves soon had the parlour as sibilant as an aviary.

Taking advantage of the lack of vigilance on the part of the old saint, the doctor ventured a joke with Eterna. 'I see we have a new chaperon,' he said. He was surprised and delighted to see a glint come into the novice's eye – until, to his chagrin, he realized that it was a glint of anger. What matter! It showed that she was at least in part human. But why did that gratify him? Quite aside from professional ethics, this disdainful creature did not in any way attract him. On the contrary! Perhaps he wanted to penetrate her unnatural indifference and send a shaft of some kind into her cold heart?

Whatever it was, after having assured himself there was no further festering in the cut, he pronounced it to be no longer dangerous, and went over to the window to make a comment on the view from it – this being his standard practice when terminating a case.

There wasn't much of a view, though. The window opened on to a small court, where at that moment the entire community of nuns was taking recreation, walking up and down the narrow asphalt paths that separated stiffly planted flower beds. 'I see the chestnuts are in bud,' he said. There wasn't much else to comment on, and he'd been surprised to see them in bud so early. But to his own ears the words didn't seem to have the proper valedictory undertones, and as he stared out at those big buds, ready to burst into leaf, he felt his heart lift at the thought that winter was over and spring well on its way. To his surprise, Eterna came and stood beside him. She looked out, too, but she still didn't smile.

'They're sticky,' she said. But although her remark may have been as inconsequential as his own, he couldn't help feeling dejected – for her – because when those sticky buds broke open and the sprawling leaves unfurled, that garden would be positively claustrophobic. The slatted seats set at regular intervals along the paths were so near to each other that there would be no more privacy out there than in the parlour.

'In the name of God, how can you be content to spend the sum of all your mortal days in this place?' he asked impulsively. Then he gave a nervous glance in the direction of the old nun in the armchair. 'Is she really deaf?' he asked.

'Stone deaf. When there is thunder and lightning, she cannot even hear the lightning,' Eterna said, almost vindictively. Then she noticed her mistake, and was overcome by the absurdity of it. 'Thunder, I mean,' she added and, yes – he could scarcely believe it – she giggled.

He laughed, too – and loudly at that. Neither of them thought of the old soul in the corner. And there was a sudden sense of freedom between them such as there might have been with any other young couple.

'Seriously,' he said, 'human relations are complicated enough at the best of times and under the best of conditions, without people locking themselves up together under the same roof for the whole of their lives. How do you stand it? Even the good Lord Himself, if we are to believe His own words, does not propose to house us all up together in His heavenly mansion!'

As he hoped she might, Eterna laughed again. 'It may be impertinent of me to say it,' he went on, 'but don't you think it is a poor thanks to your Creator to turn your back on His creation?'

'A fat lot I'd have seen of God's creation,' she said, and the unexpected colloquialism surprised him. 'I was born in this town. The oldest of ten! But for the nuns, I'd never have got anything more than elementary schooling. They educated me for nothing! And it was they who taught me to draw and to paint. There was a nun who had done her novitiate in Louvain, and she taught me all I know.' She paused, and her voice went lower. 'When I entered, I had no dowry. They took me without one because of my' – she hesitated, obviously from modesty – 'because of my gifts,' she finished, evidently unable to find another word. She blushed. The impetuosity of her outburst would have embarrassed him, too, if it were not for how amazingly that blush transformed her.

'Surely you could have got a scholarship to the College of Art, or a grant of some kind?' he said. Then he realized that he had seen nothing of her work. 'The standard is fairly high, of course,' he said hastily.

'And I am not very good, either,' she said, with a humility he would not have credited her with a few days earlier. 'My only regret is that I never saw any of the great masterpieces before I left the world – especially the moderns. You may not believe it, but I was never in the National Gallery in Dublin, much less . . .' Her voice trailed off on a note of regret.

'Oh, there's nothing much of importance in Dublin,' he lied. He didn't like the turn the conversation was taking, and he was disturbed by the sad look that had come over her face. 'Anyway, you can always get reproductions. The experts claim that detail can best be studied in photographs.'

Eterna gave a barely perceptible shrug to her shoulders. 'By students, perhaps,' she said politely, 'but I don't think anything could compensate for not being able to stand in front of the original.' The wistful expression on her face made her really beautiful. He felt it was high time for him to take his departure.

'Let's hope there will be art galleries in heaven,' he said as he took up his bag to depart. Eterna was not listening, though. Glancing back at the old soul behind them, who by her incantations had induced in herself such a state of paradisical bliss that her eyes had rolled back in her head, leaving only the whites showing, the novice detained him with a gesture.

'I'd like to show you something. Can you stay another second?' she asked breathlessly. And throwing her veil over her shoulder she seemed to send a flicker of light over his face in the way a sheet flapping on a clothes-line can seem to flash light into a sunless room. She ran out of the parlour. It entered his head fleetingly that he should leave while she was gone. But before there was time for that she was back, her face radiant.

'I found this in a wastepaper basket in one of the dormitories after the boarders went home last summer,' she said. From the thick black folds of her habit she produced a booklet. He recognized it as an ordinary catalogue from the National Gallery, but she was clasping it to her bosom with all the ardour of a saint at the stake clasping a crucifix. 'It's from the National Gallery,' she said as she placed it on a table and began to leaf through it. 'Did you know there is a Monet there? And a Sisley?' she cried. 'Have you seen them?'

Giving him no time to answer, she was feverishly searching through the illustrations. 'Ah, here it is! My favourite!' she cried, flattening out the catalogue at a colour reproduction of Monet's *River Scene*. He did not know that there was a Monet in Dublin and this one was not, as far as he knew, an important painting, but the reproduction was good, and Eterna was certainly deeply affected by it.

'How I'd love to see it,' she said. Her eyes were shining, and her parted lips showed her pearly little teeth.

He was completely swept off his feet. 'How I'd love to show it to you, Eterna,' he whispered back.

But oh, the look of shock that came on her face!

As a doctor, he could not miss it, nor mistake its implications. Neither could he fail to feel an appalling guilt at his breach of ethics. For a second that seemed as if it would last forever, they stared at each other, and from her stare he knew that to her he was some slimy, toadlike thing that had crawled out of a painting of Bosch's *Temptation of St Anthony*. Letting her treasure fall to the floor, she ran across to the armchair and, assisting the old crone to her feet, she half led, half carried her from the room like a doll.

He waited only to make sure they had vanished before he fled the place, not waiting for anyone to show him out.

It was early afternoon, but cancelling his other calls for the day, he went back to the hotel and lay on his bed in a state of shock. He thought the hour for the evening meal would never come. Although he had no appetite, he would have welcomed any gabble that would take his mind off what had occurred. Yet when the meal-time arrived, for once there was not a soul in the dining room. After barely touching his food, he went into the lounge. Two travellers were there, but they were obviously talking about something confidential, their heads close together, and he felt he could not intrude on them. Finally, he went to the hall door, thinking he might walk up the street. He saw that it was raining and he turned back into the hotel.

It was then that he saw Annie taking down her coat. Cold fish that she had seemed to him at the time, he was so desperate for company that he spoke to her. What luck for him that she had been sensible, so practical!

And now, sitting waiting for her in the car, he was filled with impatience to see her. They were intending to go home after the shops shut, but the traffic was always bad at that hour, and it occurred to him that it might be a good idea to stay and have a meal in town first. They could phone home. Ah, there she was, coming up the street towards the car with her arms full of parcels as usual. He sprang out of the car to go to meet her, when suddenly panic engulfed him again and he looked across at the gallery. But there was no sign of the crazy woman, and bolstered up by the sight of Annie advancing stoutly towards him, he relaxed again. Why should he care even if it was Eterna? If she'd gone a bit cracked, what about it? As Annie would say, she was probably headed that way from the start. People had to learn to clip their wings if they wanted to survive in this world. They had to keep their feet on the ground. That was what Annie had taught him to do – God bless her.